UNDER HER WING

Praise for Ronica Black

"Ronica Black's debut novel *In Too Deep* has everything from nonstop action and intriguing well developed characters to steamy erotic love scenes. From the opening scenes where Black plunges the reader headfirst into the story to the explosive unexpected ending, *In Too Deep* has what it takes to rise to the top. Black has a winner with *In Too Deep*, one that will keep the reader turning the pages until the very last one."—*Independent Gay Writer*

"[A]n exciting, page turning read, full of mystery, sex, and suspense."—*MegaScene*

"[A] challenging murder mystery—sections of this mixed-genre novel are hot, hot, hot. Black juggles the assorted elements of her first book with assured pacing and estimable panache."—*Q Syndicate*

"Black's characterization is skillful, and the sexual chemistry surrounding the three major characters is palpable and definitely hot-hot-hot...if you're looking for a solid read with ample amounts of eroticism and a red herring or two you're sure to find *In Too Deep* a satisfying read."—*L Word Literature*

"Black is a master at teasing the reader with her use of domination and desire. Black's first novel, *In Too Deep*, was a finalist for a 2005 Lammy...With *Wild Abandon*, the author continues her winning ways, writing like a seasoned pro. This is one romance I will not soon forget."—*Just About Write*

"The sophomore novel [*Wild Abandon*] by Ronica Black is hot, hot, hot."—*Books to Watch Out For*

By the Author

In Too Deep

Wild Abandon

Deeper

Hearts Aflame

The Seeker

Flesh and Bone

Chasing Love

Conquest

Wholehearted

The Midnight Room

Snow Angel

The Practitioner

Freedom to Love

Under Her Wing

UNDER HER WING

by

Ronica Black

2017

UNDER HER WING

ISBN 13: 978-1-63555-077-1

THIS TRADE PAPERBACK ORIGINAL IS PUBLISHED BY
BOLD STROKES BOOKS, INC.
P.O. BOX 249
VALLEY FALLS, NY 12185

FIRST EDITION: NOVEMBER 2017

CREDITS
EDITOR: CINDY CRESAP
PRODUCTION DESIGN: STACIA SEAMAN
COVER DESIGN BY TAMMY SEIDICK

Acknowledgments

Many thanks to Bold Strokes Books and my editor, Cindy Cresap. You all continue to change my life.

And to Cait, for believing.

For the love of a rescue dog. There's no love quite like it.

CHAPTER ONE

The double doors flew open, followed quickly by a rage. "I hate this school. Hate everyone here. I'm so sick of this place!" A backpack propelled from the doors to the empty library tables, the owner unseen. But as Kassandra Haden rounded the checkout counter, she knew who the voice belonged to. And she wasn't surprised.

Tony Valdez stalked inside, lifted a chair, and threw it toward the bookshelves. His young face was contorted in anger and he was nearly hyperventilating. Veins bulged in his neck and temple. He was beyond the boiling point, and the two aides that stood just inside the doors looked shocked and helpless. One finally radioed for help on her walkie-talkie. But Kassandra knew no help was coming, for one could do little with Tony. It was once again up to her.

"Tony," she said softly. But he again tossed his backpack and grabbed his head in frustration.

"I hate it here. I fucking hate it." He tried to kick a chair but missed.

Kassandra approached, arms down, palms out, and spoke calmly.

"Tony, it's okay. You're okay." She knew the young man well; they had a rapport. He was an emotional guy, a sensitive one. And when something upset him, he had a hard time controlling himself. Once he lost his temper, he was irrational.

"No, it's not okay, Ms. Haden. It's not." He flipped another chair and continued to pace.

"Tony, we don't want to have to restrain you," one of the aides said sternly.

Kassandra motioned for her to give her a moment. Sometimes the aides got too confrontational, too focused on control. That was understandable in a room full of kids. But the library was currently empty with T minus ten minutes to the last bell. Every last teacher on campus was no doubt counting down the seconds. And she knew the aides were probably eager to start their Friday evening as well. But confrontation wasn't going to help Tony now. With a soft, understanding smile, Kassandra pulled out a chair and sat at the table. Tony seemed surprised by the move, doing a double take. He was used to people keeping an arm's length, being on high alert around him. He wasn't used to normal conversation.

"Tony? Why don't you sit and tell me what's going on?"

He shook his head as he walked. "I can't. I'm mad. I'm so mad."

"It's okay to be mad," Kassandra said. "You're allowed to be mad."

"Then why is that bitch threatening to restrain me?" He didn't bother to look back at the aides he was referring to.

"You're allowed to be mad, Tony," Kassandra said. "But you can't throw things. You could hurt someone or yourself."

"Yeah, well, I don't care."

"That's not true, Tony. You do care. I know you don't want to hurt anyone."

"Just tell them to back off. They're always up my ass."

"They're backing off."

He looked back to the two women who had moved to walk behind bookshelves in the distance. He seemed to relax a little. "So, what's going on? Can you sit and talk to me?"

"I don't know, I don't know. I'm just so angry."

Kassandra noticed that he'd stopped pacing. His breathing had slowed a little and he was starting to take in his surroundings.

She changed the subject, trying to get his mind off his anger. "I finished another chapter in that book."

He lifted his head and looked at her. "Really? Did he find his wife? Is she dead? I bet she's dead."

Kassandra laughed a little. "Sit down and I'll tell you." She often shared the books she read with her students, hoping to inspire them to read. Tony was a big fan, always asking about what she was reading.

He picked up the things he'd thrown and sat down across the table. His boyish face was flushed from anger all the way up into his scalp, which she could see due to his closely shaved haircut. He clenched his hands as a thin shin of sweat became visible on his brow and upper lip.

Kassandra continued, meeting his gaze with a calm, friendly one. "Well, she's back in the picture, but the husband doesn't know it yet."

"She's alive?"

"Yes, but—"

"She's a bad guy, though, right? I knew it. I freaking knew it."

Kassandra smiled. "Yes, she's up to no good. In fact, the whole marriage was a front."

"No way!"

"Oh, yes. And she has the boy."

"Oh, my God! And he doesn't know that his kid is okay?"

Kassandra shook her head. "Nope."

"Ah, man. Ms. Haden, you gotta hurry and read. I gotta know what happens."

"I will. But you know in the meantime we need to keep reading your book." Tony struggled with reading, but she helped by reading with him. He, however, didn't care for the books at his reading level.

"My book is so lame. Because I'm stupid. Your books are better."

"Tony, you aren't stupid. You just need to practice reading. We've been over this."

"Yeah, yeah." He took a deep breath and then rested his head on his arm. Fatigue was settling over him, just as it usually did after an episode. "I'm sorry I flipped out."

"I know," she whispered. The last time it had taken fifteen minutes for him to calm down. He'd done better this time, getting his anger under control much quicker. "Next time, I think you'll do even better."

"I don't know. I'll try." He looked around. "It helps, coming in here. I hate the learning center."

Kassandra patted his hand in understanding. "I know you do." She wasn't a big fan herself. Students who had behavior issues in class often were sent to the learning center, where they were made to do their schoolwork. Unfortunately, the process wasn't working. The kids were too keyed up, angry, frustrated, bored. And putting them all in the same room...Kassandra had seen firsthand how it was a disaster just waiting to happen.

"I just get so mad." He closed his eyes for a moment and then wiped them with frustration. He didn't like to cry, but he often did when he was upset.

"Why were you mad?"

He pushed himself up and tears filled his eyes again. He avoided eye contact. "They're making fun of my ears again."

Kassandra's heart sank. He was so sensitive, and this was something that got to him every single time. "Tony, there's nothing wrong with your ears. Absolutely nothing. They're just saying that because they know it gets to you."

"Are you sure? They aren't too big?"

"No."

"You would tell me?"

"Yes."

The two aides crossed to the table. One pointed at the clock. "We need to go."

Tony groaned and stood. "Can you tell them I'm allowed to come in here? They always try and stop me."

"You are welcome here anytime, Tony, as long as you're not violent. The chair throwing—"

"I won't do it again. I promise."

"I'm going to hold you to that." Kassandra rounded the counter to shut down her computer. Tony started to push through the double doors, but he paused, looking at her. "Thanks, Ms. H."

She gave him a reassuring smile. "Have a good evening, Tony."

She watched him go, hoping he would make it home okay. Tony was often bullied, which was bad enough, but his reactions to it only made matters worse for him. She said a silent prayer for him and got busy closing down shop. It had been a long week, and she was looking forward to going home and relaxing for the weekend.

Life in the library was usually rather quiet and, honestly, often times boring. She checked books in and out and did the reshelving, she helped kids find books, helped them on the computers, and, as in Tony's case, she read with them and often told them about the books she was reading. But the quiet moments were sometimes interrupted with trouble. Students coming in and goofing off, students running from an aide, students wanting to ditch class. And then there were those like Tony. The ones who only settled down with her. The ones who needed one-on-one attention in order to calm down. She didn't know why they gravitated to her, but she took the role seriously and did her best to help. For the most part she found that the kids really just needed to know someone sincerely cared. But giving one-on-one attention to every student at the public day school for troubled kids was impossible. It often troubled her and left her feeling helpless. But in the library, there was little she could do.

The bell rang and she grabbed her purse and crossed to the doors to lock up. She cut the lights and stepped out into the brightness. Noise came at her like the sunshine, nearly overwhelming, yet warming. Kids were talking and laughing, doing their best to get off campus. Teachers stood at their assigned duty posts, sunglasses on, ID badges around their necks. They were wishing the kids a good night and weekend.

"See you at happy hour, Kassandra?" Dave Landry asked as she neared him. He taught math and the kids liked him. She stopped momentarily and stammered, always uncomfortable in these situations.

"I can't. I have plans." She felt herself flush; she was never very good with lying. She hoped he didn't notice.

"Bummer. Next time?"

"We'll see." She waved and hurried through the gates along with the mass of excited kids. She didn't like to lie, but the truth only brought more questions. Telling Dave she had no plans and that she preferred to go home to her dog, Lula, would cause him to wonder why. So she just always said she had plans or she had an appointment. It was easier that way.

The truth was she really didn't like socializing all that

much. People asked questions, and in her case, the more they knew about her the more they asked. The last happy hour she'd gone to, a question about her singlehood led to a coworker asking her out. It had made her very uncomfortable and she'd had to say no, which made things weird with him at work. Now he no longer spoke to her.

She sighed with relief as she unlocked her car and slid inside. The air was heavy with heat and she relaxed in it, still a little chilled from the AC in the library. She started her car, left the air off to let the warmth seep in some more, and checked her reflection. She looked a little tired.

She reached to put her car in reverse, but her phone rang, causing her to hold off.

The call screen showed it was her neighbor, and her heart jumped to her throat. Lauren never called unless something was wrong.

"Hello?"

"Kassandra? It's Lauren."

"What's wrong?" She tried not to panic, but they'd had a fire recently at the condominium complex, and witnessing it firsthand still left her more than a little jumpy.

"It's Lula."

Kassandra squeezed the phone. Her blood suddenly felt hot, and she put the car in reverse and began driving from the parking lot. Lula was her little terrier mix, her baby, her child. She hated leaving her home alone while she went to work, but up until now it had worked out okay. Lula was safe. She should be safe.

"Is she okay?" *Please, God, let her be okay.*

"Somebody broke into your back gate and then into your back door. I went inside to see if Lula is okay, but I can't find her."

Kassandra pulled onto the busy street and sped toward the freeway. "She's gone?" Tears nipped at her throat as her heart raced. *Please, God, no. She's so little, so innocent, so timid.*

"Harry just came home and said he spotted her out by the field across the road. He tried to get her, but she ran from him. He's going to go look again. I can't because I'm waiting for the police. I can't tell you how much they took. It's a mess."

"I don't care about that," she said. "I'm just worried about Lula." Lula was a rescue, and though she'd come a long way as far as overcoming her fears, she was still afraid of strangers. It was unlikely she would come to anyone, even if they were trying to help. "I'm on my way."

She ended the call and accelerated onto the freeway. Tears ran down her face, hot, wet, frustrating. She wiped them away, trying to be strong. She had to think, had to focus. Lula needed her.

She'd adopted her three years ago from the Humane Society after her dachshund passed away. She really hadn't thought about getting another dog so soon, but her friends encouraged her to go, just to see if any dog grabbed her heart. She'd walked up and down the aisles, dogs yipping and barking in their pens. Most had been large dogs, too big for life in a two-bedroom condo. But then, at the very last kennel, she'd seen Lula, curled in a ball, trembling with fear. Kassandra's heart had bled for her right away, and she'd asked to see her. The volunteer had put on gloves, taken her out, and brought them into a small room. She'd handed Lula to her, and that had sealed the deal. Lula had curled up on her, lightly kissed her chin, and wagged her little tail. She hoped she'd be able to get some of those kisses again soon.

Kassandra pulled off at her exit and sped toward home. Lula was a great little dog and she wasn't about to lose her.

Instead of turning down her street, she drove straight to

the field where Harry had said he'd seen her. She parked along the curb, killed the engine, and threw open the door. Harry was nearby in the desert field and he trotted over, meeting her halfway.

"I don't see her now," he breathed, squinting into the sun. "Last time I saw her was there." He pointed to the brick fencing of the homes built next to the field. "She was walking along there, headed farther in. I called her and she turned back, but she wouldn't come to me. So I ran home, got some treats and a leash, and came back out. I thought maybe she'd still be here."

Kassandra scanned the large desert field, looking for anything white. Her heart sank when she saw nothing but desert. Harry looked with her, and she could tell he felt bad. She placed a hand on his shoulder and thanked him for trying.

"I'm going to go search the streets," she said, hurrying back to her vehicle. She climbed in and headed down the street next to the field. She drove slowly, eyes keen. She did the same on the next street and the next. And then she came upon the golf course. She stopped her car, her body filling with dread. If Lula was exploring the golf course, there's no telling where she'd end up.

Her phone rang as she pulled away, feeling helpless.

"Kassandra, the police are here," Lauren said. "Are you close to home?"

She drove home slowly, not wanting to face what lay ahead. Her home had been broken into and Lula was gone. What was she going to do? She pulled into her parking space and sat for a moment. Her body wanted to cry, but she wouldn't let herself lose control. Not yet. There was too much to do.

She stared at the police cruiser parked next to her and said a silent prayer, not for herself or for her home, but for Lula.

CHAPTER TWO

Jayden Beaumont loved to hear a dog bark with excitement. A good, strong bark of enthusiasm meant health and vigor, a thirst for life, an insatiable curiosity. Barks like those were music to her ears. She could hear them well before she approached the kennels, and she smiled. The August day was hot, beautiful, and alive with sunshine. Her dogs were thriving and safe and she…well, she felt damn good.

She opened the door to the air-conditioned kennels and whistled a hello to dog after dog as she walked. Each and every one was special to her, some of them rescued from the streets by her personally. She took them in, nurtured them, kept them safe, and then adopted them out to forever families. She'd saved hundreds of dogs over the years, and her mission was far from complete. There were hundreds more out there who needed a safe place. And as long as she was breathing, she'd be there for them.

She broke out in song, bellowing loudly as she often did when walking the kennels. The dogs often howled with her, loving the old Sinatra songs more than she did. She sang as she moved, spreading her arms wide, encouraging the dogs to chime in. Over her handheld radio she heard the voices start.

"Oh God, Beaumont's singing again."

"Make it stop!"

"I wish the howling would drown her out."

She smiled, finished the song, took a bow, and stopped at the last kennel.

A border collie mix she called Cooper lay in his bed with his ears back.

She unlatched the door and stepped inside. "Hey, Coop, did you like the song? I sang that one just for you."

She knelt and held out a treat. He came to her cautiously, tail wagging. A few of the dogs next to them still howled, but Cooper seemed okay. She was trying to get him used to noise and people. "Good boy," she said as he took the treat and licked her hand. She gave him a scratch just under his ear and he kissed her face. "That's a good boy, Coop."

He'd come a long way in the two weeks she'd had him. She'd found him on a destroy list at another shelter. They'd said he was too fearful to rehabilitate. She'd gone to meet him and was moved right away by his beauty. He was tricolored, black, white, and brown, with one blue eye. His history had been unknown and Jayden suspected he'd been mistreated. So she'd sat in his kennel for an hour and waited him out. Eventually, he'd relaxed and lain down. She'd spoken softly to him, and every once in a while, moved a little closer. She'd pulled a liver treat from her pocket and tossed it to him. He'd eaten it right away. And over the course of another hour, she'd placed more treats in front of him, encouraging him to come closer. When he finally took a treat from her hand and then licked her fingers, she'd slipped the leash on him and eased him out of the kennel with more treats. She'd taken him home to her no kill shelter, and she'd worked with him a couple of hours every day since then.

Cooper licked her face again and she clipped on the leash. She rose carefully, encouraging him with light words. His body relaxed and he wagged his tail as she opened the door and exited. He followed on her heels closely as they headed outside.

The afternoon sun was still bright, and she knew in the August heat they wouldn't be able to stay outside for very long. She opened the gate to one of the fenced-in grass lots and let him loose. He flew off the leash and sprinted down to the end, grabbed his favorite tennis ball, and sprinted back.

Jayden laughed, remembering how when he'd first arrived he'd been skittish outdoors, uncomfortable leaving her side. Now he was relaxing enough to play, and it warmed her heart.

"Drop it," she said, grinning. Cooper sat and dropped the ball. Then he stuck his rear in the air and wagged his tail, anticipating.

"Ask for it. Ask for it, Cooper!" He barked and she threw the ball as hard as she could. Cooper tore off after it, clawing up grass as he ran.

"He's come a long way."

Jayden turned as one of her teen staff members entered the lot. Gus was seventeen and nearly six foot five. With a genuine smile and dark hair like hers that often fell over his eyes, he was a lady-killer. Like Cooper, he'd come a long way as well since she'd first met him at fourteen. He'd been in a bad car accident, one that he caused on a joyride. He'd done a stint in juvie and still had the yearning for trouble, so his PO had recommended him to Jayden.

"He reminds me of you," Jayden said, once again tossing the ball for Cooper.

"Me?" He sank his hands in his pockets and looked sheepish.

"Yeah, you know, good-looking, lots of energy, a little afraid at first."

"I have never been afraid."

Jayden scoffed. "Yes, you have. Remember how timid you were your first few weeks? Scared to death of us and of returning to juvie?"

He kicked the grass with his black Chucks.

"Maybe. It was mostly about juvie."

"Uh-huh. Tough guy." She grinned. Gus was one of ten troubled teens on her staff. She believed in rehabilitation, having once been a teen in trouble herself.

She rubbed Cooper vigorously and threw the ball for him again. Voices came from behind, and she turned to see a blond boy, about ten or eleven years old, walking with what appeared to be his mother. Faith, another one of Jayden's teen staff members, was showing them around.

"Mom, look!" the boy said, running up to the fence. He pointed to Cooper and bounced on his feet. "I like this one."

Jayden crossed to him, Cooper trotting up behind her. "You like Cooper?"

"Yeah, he's great. I like the way he looks and how fast he runs. Mom, can I have him?"

His mother offered a gentle smile. "He's wonderful, John, but we haven't seen any of the others yet."

Jayden gave the same commands again to Cooper. He followed and then took off after the ball once again.

"He's smart!" John said. "See, Mom?"

"Cooper's not quite ready for adoption yet," Jayden said. "He needs to be socialized more. He's very shy."

John didn't falter and his eyes didn't leave Cooper. "How long?"

"A few more weeks."

"I can wait," John said. "Can you hold him for us?"

"John, let's go look at the other dogs."

"I don't want to. I want him."

Jayden called Cooper and clipped on his leash. "Tell you

what," she said, looking at John. "Let's take a walk through the kennels so you can see the other dogs. Then, if you still want Cooper, we'll go sit down and talk about it."

John seemed to think for a moment. He nodded. "Okay."

Jayden smiled. "Great, follow me." She and Cooper left the lot and led the way to the kennels. John ran to walk next to her, his eyes still trained on Cooper who walked at her heels. Faith and Gus headed for the front office to help other guests.

"Can I pet him?"

"Not yet." The dogs began barking before they entered. "It gets kind of loud," she said as she opened the door. "Really loud."

John plugged his ears as they stepped inside. Cooper's ears went back and his tail lowered. He didn't like the kennels. Jayden called out to the dogs and turned to John and his mother. "Each one of these dogs has been vet checked, vaccinated, and spayed or neutered. All of them are friendly, loving animals just looking for a good home and wonderful new life."

They began walking past individual kennels, looking at each dog. "Where do you get them?" John's mother asked.

"It varies," Jayden said. "Some are found on the street or in the desert. Others we get from animal control. We also get some from vet clinics and some are surrendered by owners. Cooper here, I got from another kennel. He was about to be put down."

"Really?" John said.

"Why?" his mother asked.

"He's fearful." Jayden led them down another aisle. "He's already come a long way. A few more weeks and he'll be okay. If he's not, then he stays on with me."

"You keep some of the dogs?"

"If need be. All eventually find the right home. But some

I've kept for years, waiting for the right family. I call them my own."

"How many dogs do you have?" John asked.

"Seven of my own. And sometimes over fifty in the kennels."

John turned to his mother. "Can I have seven, Mom?"

She laughed. "Um, no."

John continued to look at the dogs as they walked up and down the aisles. He saw a couple that he commented on, but mostly he kept his eyes on Cooper.

When they reached the end, Jayden stopped at the door. He spoke before she could ask.

"I still want Cooper."

Jayden liked his determination. The first dog she'd brought home as a kid was due to her determination. His mother, though, sighed. She looked to Jayden and then to John and then back to Jayden.

"Are you serious about letting John have him?"

Jayden walked them through another door and into the front office. The quiet was welcome, even if it was disturbed by ringing phones and busy voices.

Jayden rounded her desk, encouraged Cooper to lie on a dog bed next to her, and then motioned for mother and son to sit.

"Please," she said as she too sat. She got right to the point. "Cooper is a special dog. He's very intelligent, very energetic, and he's still a little afraid. We need to work on this before I consider him okay for adoption. He should be fine in a few weeks, but if he isn't, I'll have to keep him here."

"So I might not get him?" John asked.

"Right. But in the meantime, if you really want him, you can actually help."

"I can?"

"You can help socialize him. Spend time with him, let him get to trust you, play with him, take him on walks. What do you say?"

He grinned from ear to ear. "I say yes!"

His mother still looked unconvinced. "Has this dog ever bitten anyone?"

Jayden opened a drawer and thumbed through some files. When she found Cooper's, she handed it over. "To my knowledge, no. He was found in the desert, starved and filthy. He ran from everyone trying to help him. When he was finally caught, he didn't growl or snap. He just cowered. The shelter I got him from said the same. He's never snapped or shown any aggression no matter how frightened he is. And John will always be in my presence."

She exhaled and appeared to relax a little. John smiled. "Can I pet him now?"

Jayden stood, rounded the desk, and picked up Cooper's leash. He stood and turned.

"Stay right there but relax your hands. Let them fall to your sides."

John did and Jayden moved closer, encouraging Cooper with soft words. She reached out and handed John a liver treat and told him to call the dog softly.

"Here, Cooper. Come here, boy."

Jayden moved closer and knelt next to John. Cooper came slowly, lying down and crawling up to Jayden. Jayden tapped John's hand and Cooper sniffed it. John opened his hand and Cooper took the treat.

"Good boy," Jayden said, rewarding him with gentle strokes. "Now, offer him your hand, let him smell you again."

John did and Cooper licked him. He inched closer. John sat very still, letting Cooper get comfortable.

"Good job, John." She placed another treat in his hand and Cooper took it. John praised him, and again Cooper licked his hand. This time, though, he nudged him a bit and Jayden smiled.

"He wants you to pet him."

"Really?"

"Go ahead." She took his hand and placed it along his neck. "Very softly."

John stroked him gently and cooed at him with kind words. He was very good with Cooper, very calm, and Jayden was impressed.

"Can you come back next week?" she asked, looking to Mom.

"Can I, Mom?"

"I suppose."

John smiled. Jayden patted him on the back. "Okay, call me first, make sure I'm here." She handed him her card. "See you then."

John and his mother stood, shook her hand, and walked out. John called good-bye to Cooper from the door just before pushing out into the sun.

"Cute kid," said Allie, her friend and colleague for over ten years. "Think he'll be back?"

Jayden returned to her chair and Cooper to his bed. "If his mom lets him, he'll be here."

Allie began organizing a stack of files on her desk. For the moment, it was quiet. No families, no phone calls. Jayden knew it wouldn't last long.

"You have four messages," Allie said. "They're on your desk."

"Only four?" She usually had eight or more.

Allie gave her a grunt. "You're lucky I take care of most it for you."

"Love you, Allstar." Jayden grinned at her. She called her Allstar because she was priceless around the Angel's Wings kennel. Life would not continue without Allie.

Jayden looked over her messages. Two were from another kennel. They had two dogs for her because they were now full. One message was from one of her vets who'd just performed surgery on a dog that had been hit by a car. She wanted to know if Jayden would take her. The last message was from a woman who had recently adopted a pet. She worked for a local news station and she wanted to do a story on Angel's Wings.

"Did you see that message from the news channel lady?" Allie asked.

"I did." Public attention was great, but it was also strenuous. Attention brought in more people, and some of those people weren't ready for a dog, but they just didn't know it yet. Jayden, unfortunately, had to be the one to tell them. She saw all her dogs all the way through, and that meant interviewing and going to the home to check it out before each and every adoption. And she'd seen more than a few homes that weren't dog appropriate.

"She's anxious to come by," Allie said. "Said she was really impressed with us."

Jayden picked up the phone to return the calls. Normally, she had to return calls on the fly because she was so busy, but for the moment she had some time. They'd adopted out four dogs so far for the day, and she was allowed to let the contentment wash over her a bit. Taking time to enjoy the fulfillment of her job was often rare, but it did help her sleep at night. As she dialed the number to one of the other rescues, her cell phone, which had a dog barking ringtone, rang on her hip. She recognized the number right away. It was Mel, her best friend.

"Mel," she said, turning to stroke Cooper. "What is it?"

Mel had been out approving the last family to adopt. Jayden trusted her completely.

"I just got a call from a hysterical woman. Her home was broken into and the dog got out. Little terrier mix. She can't find her, and apparently the dog is a rescue and still afraid of strangers."

Jayden leaned forward, alert. "She near the desert?" She immediately thought of coyotes.

"Mainly homes and a large golf course. We haven't had any calls about a lost white terrier, have we?"

Jayden looked up at the intake board. Only one new one brought in so far today. A German shepherd mix.

"No, we haven't."

"I really feel for this lady. Can you keep your ears to the ground for me?"

"Sure. Make sure she calls other rescues as well."

Jayden ended the call and looked to Cooper. She wished she could help the woman and every dog who needed it, but she could only do so much. It pained her to acknowledge that, and she still had a hard time living by that rule. Working long into the night and going on early morning calls was her mantra. But from time to time she had to slow down and rest. Mel and the others insisted on it, sometimes hiding her car keys so she'd have to stay at home rather than go out on call after call.

"Hey, Allie. Keep your eyes open for a little white terrier mix. She's lost and someone may call about her."

"She microchipped?"

"I don't know. But Mel knows the lady. I guess her home was broken into today and the dog got out."

Allie looked crestfallen. "That's terrible."

Jayden nodded. "Yes, it is." She couldn't imagine coming home to find her dogs gone and her place ransacked. How awful.

Jayden took a moment to thank her lucky stars for all she had. She had her shelter, her rescues, her own adopted dogs, her home, which sat on the same property as her kennel, and her friends. Life was good. But as she knew from dealing with rescues, it wasn't always good for others.

Allie's phone rang and Jayden's ears piqued. It was a rescue call. Her heart rate kicked up just as it always did when they got a call. She never knew what she was going to find or who was involved. Allie hung up and crossed the room to Jayden. The look on her face was stoic, and Jayden always hated that she couldn't read her. But Allie was strong and always remained calm. It's what helped keep the place going.

"Is it bad?" Jayden asked.

"Brad wasn't able to go into too much detail. He just said there's a dog stuck in a drainage pipe out near Sun City. He's waiting on you before he calls the fire department. You better hurry."

Jayden stood and grabbed her keys. She slid on her cell phone and grabbed two bottles of water from the mini fridge behind her desk.

"Did Brad say if the dog was hurt?"

"He can't tell." Brad was a good friend from the Emergency Animal Rescue. He sometimes gave Jayden the heads-up on dogs needing help. Allie handed her the paper with the address.

"Will you take Cooper?" Jayden gave her his leash. "And if the news lady calls back, tell her we're interested. I'll get back to her as soon as I can."

Jayden hurried across the office to the double doors. She pushed out into the waning sun and headed for her truck.

Another dog was in trouble.

It was time to go to work.

CHAPTER THREE

H ere, have some wine, sweetie."
Kassandra took the wineglass from her friend Wendy
with a trembling hand. She sipped it cautiously at first but then
took a few good swallows. She was at Wendy and Katelynn's
house, having packed up a few of her things from her home to
stay a few nights. She was a wreck, and her two dear friends
were trying their best to comfort her.

"We'll put up more flyers first thing in the morning,"
Katelynn said, sliding over the hummus and veggies on the
coffee table.

Kassandra eyed the food with distaste. She couldn't eat a
bite. Her mind kept going to Lula. Where was she? What was
happening to her? It was torturous.

"I just can't stop thinking about her."

Wendy scooted closer to her on the couch and took her
hand. "I know, I know. You've had a very traumatic day. I think
you're in a bit of shock, to be honest." Her blue eyes shined
and Katelynn joined them, hugging Wendy from behind. They
were an adorable couple and Kassandra's closest friends. The
only ones who could get her out of the house.

"Someone will find her, Kassie. Someone good."

Kassandra dabbed her eyes. "Her tag, the phone number looks worn. I bet they can't read it."

"I'm sure it's fine, honey." Wendy patted her hand. "Try to think positively."

"I know what you need," Katelynn said. "Some more wine and a good movie. How about your favorite?"

Kassandra couldn't. Not even *Love Actually* could cheer her up tonight. "I think I'm just going to go to bed."

Wendy looked at the clock. Kassandra knew it was early. But she just needed to lie down and breathe.

"Don't you want to wait up to see if anyone calls?" Wendy asked.

Kassandra thumbed the screen on her phone. Nothing. Her stomach sank. She couldn't bear to see the bare screen anymore. It was driving her mad.

She slid it over to Wendy. "Wake me if someone calls."

"You know you're welcome here for as long as you need," Katelynn said softly. "So don't worry about that."

Kassandra nodded. She rose and crossed to the hallway. Her eyes adjusted to the dim light and she entered the bedroom in the near darkness. She sat on the bed and removed her shoes. She thought of her home and how it had looked like a hurricane had gone through it. The burglar had taken her laptop, her stereo, and some jewelry. He'd also made off with some priceless family heirlooms.

She sighed and ran her hands through her hair. She glanced back at the bed and wished that she had someone in her life. She thought of how nice it would be to curl up in someone's arms right then and drift off to sleep. More than anything, she just needed someone to tell her it was going to be okay.

Wendy and Katelynn had that. They had a wonderful marriage. Fourteen years strong. They were always trying to get her to date, but she just didn't want to let anyone in. People made promises they couldn't keep. Said things they didn't mean. She'd been through all that before with her father, and she just wasn't strong enough to go through any more of it.

She lay back and stared at the ceiling. She didn't need people. Not when she had Lula.

She closed her eyes as tears ran down her cheeks. She'd had such a range of emotions surge through her the past few hours that now her body was limp with fatigue and her mind cloudy with fog. She calmed her breathing and allowed her troubled mind to shut down. It didn't take long before she was fast asleep.

❖

"Kassie, Kassie, wake up."

Kassandra opened her eyes to find Wendy leaning over her, hand on her shoulder. Kassandra's eyes drifted closed again and the events of the day before seeped into her mind. She bolted upright.

"What is it? Did someone call? Is she okay?"

Wendy sat next to her on the bed. She took her hand and spoke softly. "A cop called. The one investigating your break-in. He wants you to call him back. And a shelter called. They think they have Lula."

"Oh, my God. Oh, my God." She palmed her chest and stood, so grateful she thought she might faint. Lula. She was found.

Wendy held fast to her hand. "Kassie, that's not all."

"What do you mean?" Just as soon as her heart had soared to the ceiling, it now plummeted to the floor with fear. "She's okay, isn't she?"

Wendy nodded. "She is, but she's been through a lot."

"What does that mean?"

"She was found in a drainage pipe. They don't know how long she was in there. It took a while to get her out."

"Please, just tell me she's okay." She wiped angrily at a tear.

"They took her to an emergency clinic where she spent the night. She's unharmed, but she was very weak and dehydrated."

Kassandra began searching for her clothes. "I have to go. I have to go get her."

Wendy stood and placed a hand on her shoulder. "Kassie, they said she's okay. A shelter took her in because they had your contact information. She's resting comfortably there. Why don't you at least take a shower and have some breakfast? You didn't eat last night and—"

Kassandra lifted her suitcase onto the bed. Her heart still fluttered even though she knew Lula was okay and safe. "She must be so afraid."

"Kassie, please listen. We're a little worried about you." Wendy squeezed her hand.

Kassandra looked at her and stopped pulling out clothes. She let out a long, shaky breath. "I'll take a shower, maybe have some toast."

Wendy smiled. "Thank you. I'll get breakfast ready and then I'll get ready to go with you."

"I can go alone," Kassandra said. Wendy and Katelynn had already done so much for her. And besides, she knew she'd probably lose it when she saw Lula. She wanted to do that alone.

"Are you sure?"

Kassandra nodded. "I am. I'm used to, you know, being alone."

Wendy was silent for a moment. "You know, you're not

alone, Kassie. Katelynn and I, we're here for you. We can be with you today too. Just say the word."

"I know, and I can't thank you enough. I just—I need to do this alone. And I need to take Lula home and get things in order."

Wendy offered another soft smile. "Okay. But I'm at least going to make you breakfast."

She walked through the doorway, leaving Kassandra alone to shower and get ready. Kassandra took her clothes and toiletries to the bathroom, where she quickly showered and dressed. Then she zipped up her suitcase and headed for the living room.

"I made you toast and eggs," Wendy said, setting a plate on the table in the cozy kitchen nook. Katelynn swept into the room, satin bathrobe swaying behind her as she moved.

"Good morning, loves," she said, giving Kassandra a gentle squeeze and Wendy a lingering kiss. "Did you get the good news, Kassie?" She smiled broadly and came to sit across from her.

"I did," Kassandra bit into her toast.

"Thank God, right?" She reached for her hand and patted it with excitement. Her brown eyes were deep and soulful and her thick auburn hair was pulled back into a loose ponytail. "I told you good people would find her." She sipped her coffee. "So when can we go get her?"

"Actually," Wendy said as she brought two more plates to join them, "Kassie wants to go alone."

Katelynn looked a little surprised. "Oh, okay. But you're bringing her back here, right?"

Kassandra finished chewing. Wendy was silently eating, but Katelynn was looking at her with concern.

"I think I should take her home, to where she's familiar. I have to start putting things back together sometime."

"Well, we can come help. We'll have it done in no time. Good as new. And I've got that number for you, you know, the guy with the security company?"

Kassandra took a drink of her juice. She felt bad, knowing her friends just wanted to help. But she had to pull back now. Back into herself. It was the way she survived.

"Thank you, Katelynn, for offering, but I need to do it alone. Now that I know Lula is okay, I just need to go home and regroup. Get things settled."

Katelynn lowered her eyes and then looked to Wendy. "We understand."

"We just worry, Kassie. You won't let anyone in—"

"I let you guys in. All the time." She did; she loved them, trusted them.

"Only so far," Katelynn said. "Then you pull back again. Like now."

"You don't have to be alone, sweetie," Wendy said. "We mean that."

"I know, but—"

"Why won't you date?" Katelynn asked. "Remember that guy Brian? He's really nice and cute and—"

"I'm just not interested."

"Why?"

"Because—" She stopped. What was her reason? Did she have one?

Katelynn and Wendy were watching her, their hands entwined.

"Because I just don't want to." That should be reason enough.

"Will you at least give him a chance?" Katelynn asked. "Meet us for happy hour? It won't be a date, just a group of friends meeting for drinks."

"I don't know." She pushed away her food and wiped her mouth. "I really should get going."

Katelynn and Wendy stood. Katelynn came around the table and hugged her. "Aw, shit, honey, I didn't mean to scare you away. I just want so badly for you to let someone in. If not us, someone else. Someone who you'll let love you. Because you deserve love so much."

Wendy embraced her too, a double dose of hugging. "We love you," Wendy said.

"I love you, too." Kassandra pulled away and tried to smile. But on the inside she felt panic, like they were trying to trap her. She didn't want to date Brian or anyone else. She didn't want to let anyone in. Her reasons were her own.

She crossed to the living room, suitcase in hand. "I'll call you," she said. "And thank you. For yesterday."

"You better call us," Wendy said, handing over the information on the shelter and another name and number. "Let us know how the two of you are doing." She wrapped an arm around Katelynn's waist. "And don't forget to call that policeman. Officer Paul Jensen. He needs to ask you some more questions."

"I will." She gave them another smile and turned to walk out the door.

CHAPTER FOUR

I'm telling you, Beaumont, you shouldn't have blown her off. She was really into you," Mel said as they both carried in large bags of dog food. Jayden set hers on the storage shelves in the back of the warehouse. She wiped her brow and knelt to organize the cans of food next to the dry food.

"I didn't blow her off. I just—"

"Did absolutely nothing."

Jayden laughed. "Well, to be honest, I kind of forgot she was there." Despite the AC being on next door in the kennels, the air was stifling in the warehouse. "I hate how hot it gets in here. We need circulation or something." Cooling the kennel in the Arizona summer heat was costly, so they kept the inside kennel temp between seventy-eight and eighty degrees with floor fans added for extra circulation. People from out of town often thought it was too hot until they walked indoors from a hundred and seventeen degrees. Then eighty degrees felt nice. Really nice with the fans. But to cool the warehouse would cost a small fortune. "What about some large floor fans for in here?"

"Don't change the subject." Mel unloaded the last bag and pulled down the door to the truck. She pounded on the side, letting the driver know he could leave. "Besides, it always gets hot when we open the big doors."

Mel knelt alongside her and grabbed cans to place on the shelves. "Seriously, why did you blow her off? I put weeks in trying to get this woman for you."

"That's just it, Mel, I don't need you to get a woman for me. I do fine on my own." She looked her in the eye, but she knew she wasn't buying it.

"Yeah, you do fine all right. You can have anyone you want, yet lately there doesn't seem to be anybody good enough."

"Oh, ouch," Jayden said. "Now you're making me out to be a snob."

"Hey, if the shoe fits."

"I happen to want something serious this time around. Someone with substance. Someone who hasn't slept with more than half the lesbians in town."

"Since when?"

Jayden finished and stood, running her hands through her thick, short hair. "Since now."

"So there's no chance you'll go out with her again?"

"With who? Her? No. And I don't need you fixing me up anymore."

Mel stood alongside her and they walked through the doors to the front office. "Uh, yeah, about that. It might be a little too late."

Jayden turned as she entered. "What do you mean?"

Mel's face drained of color as if she'd been caught cheating on a test.

"Jayden?" Allie called from the front counter.

"Yes?" Jayden crossed the room to stand next to her.

"Jayden, this is Kassandra Haden."

Jayden followed Allie's gaze, eager to see what was going on. The office was busy with more than a handful of people talking with her staff members. A blond woman stepped into her line of sight in the bright sunlight, and Jayden felt her breath catch. Their eyes locked and Jayden forgot to speak, too taken with her quiet beauty.

"Jayden?" Allie nudged her.

"Sorry?" Jayden couldn't look away. She was being drawn into her, inescapably so.

"She's here about—"

And suddenly Jayden knew. She tore her eyes away to look back at Mel, who had somehow disappeared.

"I think I know what this is about." The woman was too beautiful, too perfect. Boy, Mel had really gone out of her way this time.

"I'm Kassandra," the woman said, outstretching her hand.

Jayden gave her a crooked smile and took her hand softly. It was soft, warm. Yet the woman had a nice firm grip. Jayden studied her stylish short haircut, her lovely rose-colored lips, and her skin...so smooth and supple looking. Olive in tone with a bit of a shimmer like she'd just applied a creamy lotion.

"Why don't you follow me?" Jayden swung open the waist-high gate. Kassandra entered and followed her across the room and back to the doors that led to the kennels, the medical room, and the warehouse. Jayden pushed through into the area that led to the medical room. She took Kassandra's hand to walk her farther inside. When she was sure they were alone and out of sight, Jayden pulled her close.

"I've got to tell you I was against this, but now—I mean seeing you—you're breathtaking, and the whole quiet, humble thing, Jesus, you're right on. You're single, right?"

Kassandra was searching her eyes and she seemed to hesitate. "Yes, I am, but—"

Jayden grew alarmed. "Are you sure? Because I don't do married or taken. I'm not into that."

"I understand, but—"

"So you're single?"

Kassandra looked frustrated. "Yes, but I really don't see—"

"Great. And you're an animal lover, right?"

"Yes, but really—"

"I can't tell you how long I've waited to be moved by someone. That instant chemistry you always hear about. I was beginning to think it didn't exist. And Mel, she really did it. How did she find you? Where did she find you? Dear God, I want to know so I can go there all the time." She leaned in and inhaled the scent from her neck. "God, you smell good." She felt Kassandra shudder and take in a shaky breath.

The intensity between them was palpable. Kassandra was flushed, and Jayden could see the pulse jumping in her neck. She kept trying to speak, but the words wouldn't come. Jayden was nearly speechless herself.

"Where have you been hiding?" Jayden said into her ear. She placed her hands on her hips and looked into her eyes. "Who are you, Kassandra? I want to know everything. Every last detail. I want to read the book of your life, from page one to infinity." She wanted so badly to kiss her, but she wanted to take it slow, despite her immediate attraction. She took a deep breath and stepped back. First things first.

"Dinner," she said. "Can you meet me for dinner? I can get free after six."

"I—" Kassandra said. "I think there's been some sort of mistake."

"No, not this time. No trouble, no drama. Not with you. Please."

"I'm pretty drama free," she said, giving a sarcastic laugh.

"Good, great." Jayden smiled. She took her hand. "Because I would really love to get to know you."

Kassandra blinked quickly and gently retrieved her hand. She looked away. Jayden downshifted once again, panicked.

"What is it?"

"I'm a little—unsure what is happening," Kassandra said. Jayden realized the problem. "It's me. You're not into me." She rubbed her forehead in embarrassment. "Damn. I'm so sorry. I came on way too strong—"

Kassandra crossed her arms over her chest and rubbed them as if she were cold. She looked equally embarrassed. "I-I'm not here for you." She met her eyes briefly and looked away.

"Sorry?" Was she here for Mel? Allie? What was going on?

"I'm here for my dog."

"Your dog?" Jayden couldn't think fast enough. It was like she had missed out on the last five minutes altogether. She couldn't put the pieces where they belonged.

"Her name is Lula. She was stuck in a drainage pipe."

Jayden felt as if she'd been slapped. She stepped back and willed her clenched heart to beat. "Oh, no." She covered her mouth. "Oh God. I thought—"

"Can I see her now, please?"

Jayden kept staring. She heard the words, but she didn't seem to understand them. "Sorry?"

"My dog," she said, her flush becoming more prominent. "I'd really like to see her."

Jayden heated. Her mind spun and she still couldn't quite grasp what was real and what wasn't. "Mel didn't send you?"

"I spoke to a Mel yesterday, but no, I'm not here for... you."

Jayden felt about two inches tall. She wanted to run, and yet she wanted to faint dead away. Anything to get out of this moment. She swallowed hard and cleared her throat.

"Of course." She headed toward the kennels, then halted and went for the medical room door. She was mixed up, confused, and where the hell was Mel? She wanted to pummel her. When they entered the quiet room, Jayden went straight for the little white terrier. She opened her kennel door and lifted her gently. The dog had been sleeping and she trembled a little in Jayden's arms.

"It's okay," Jayden said softly. She turned and offered her to Kassandra. "She's been resting."

Kassandra gasped and took her and hugged her close. The dog perked up and wagged her tail. She assaulted Kassandra with kisses.

Jayden smiled, her heart warmed at the reunion. She still felt awkward and ashamed. "She's very sweet," she said, knowing she couldn't say anything to make her forget what had happened.

Kassandra spoke softly to her dog, kissing her and stroking her short fur. Tears streamed down her face. "Thank you," she finally said.

"It was our pleasure." Jayden nearly hit herself. Could she sound any sleazier? Should she say anything at all or would it all sound like she was coming on to her? Where was Mel? She was going to kill her. Always asking eligible women to stop by the shelter to flirt with her. It had gone too far, and now she'd made a complete ass out of herself.

"Is she okay?" Kassandra asked, doing her best to look her over.

Jayden nodded. "She was scared and dehydrated, but that was the extent of it." Jayden didn't tell her that she was the one who had crawled in the pipe to get her. She didn't tell her that she'd spent hours with her at the medical clinic soothing her, making sure she was okay. She didn't tell her that she'd bathed her and then let her sleep with her in her own bed to help ease her fear. None of that mattered now. All that mattered was that Lula was okay and back in the loving arms of her owner.

Kassandra hugged Lula closely and looked back to Jayden. "What do I owe you?"

Jayden was surprised at the question. She'd rescued many dogs, and unfortunately, she didn't see many get reunited with their loving owners. Seeing that alone was priceless. "Not a thing. We're good."

"Well, I insist on making a donation to your shelter. Will you take a personal check?"

Jayden saw the look in her eyes. She wasn't going to take a polite no for an answer. And Jayden wasn't about to argue with her.

"That's really nice of you. And very much appreciated."

"It's the least I can do. You have no idea what she means to me."

Jayden understood all too well. "I'm just glad we could help."

Kassandra looked at her briefly, as if searching her for authenticity. She glanced away before Jayden could tell if she thought she'd found it.

Voices came from beyond the med room door, and when it opened, two teen staff members entered all smiles.

"Ms. H.!" Gus said, throwing out his arms for an embrace.

"I knew it was you," Billy said as he joined in on the hug. "I saw you in the parking lot and I said that looks just like Ms. Haden."

"He did," said Gus. "He came running up to me in the kennels like, yo, Ms. H. is here. And I was like, what? And he was like, yeah, man, I'm serious. So I had to come see for myself."

Kassandra appeared to be overwhelmed. She smiled broadly and looked from boy to boy, wiping a tear from her eye. "This is such a crazy day," she said, laughing softly.

Jayden once again felt ashamed at her behavior. But she swallowed back her embarrassment and watched the interaction.

"You guys got so tall," Kassandra said, wiping away another tear.

Jayden's curiosity was piqued. Was Kassandra a teacher? She must be a good one to have impressed her boys. They were hard in ways other kids weren't. They'd had tough lives, and many had the emotional and physical scars to prove it.

"You all know each other?" Jayden asked, her curiosity getting the best of her. Just who was Kassandra Haden?

The boys turned and Gus spoke. "She's only like the best teacher ever."

"We had her in middle school," Billy said. "Man, I hated that school. You were the only reason I kept going."

Kassandra's blush reached her cheeks, and she reached out and squeezed his arm. "You two are certainly missed," she said. "Please tell me you're still going to school."

"They are," Jayden said. "They can't work here unless they are enrolled and keep at least a C average."

Gus waved her off. "Those are Beaumont's rules. Worse than the school."

"What was that, Gus?" Jayden said playfully.

"Beaumont keeps us out of trouble," Billy said. "And out of juvie."

"Oh," Kassandra said. "So you work here for her?"

"Yeah," Gus said. "She cool most of the time."

Jayden laughed. "Keep talking, Gus, and you'll be back on dog detail."

"See what I mean? She threatening me with dog shit now. Anytime I get out of line, she makes me clean up dog shit."

Kassandra laughed a little. "Does it work?"

Jayden slapped him on the back. "It absolutely works." She pushed open the door and allowed Kassandra to exit first. Then they crossed to the front office. The boys followed, talking eagerly to their former teacher. Jayden had to admit she was impressed. Kassandra obviously had had an impact on the boys. But mostly, she was still reeling from the impact Kassandra had had on her. No one else had ever moved her like Kassandra. And she'd even made a complete fool of herself over her. Just who was she? And more importantly, how could she make things better and get to know her?

CHAPTER FIVE

Kassandra listened to the boys chatter about their lives, about school, and about the shelter. She was a little overwhelmed at all the attention, but she was extremely happy to see them again. She sat in the chair Jayden Beaumont offered her across from her desk. Kassandra smiled politely at her, but she averted her eyes quickly, too afraid she would see the fire in her that she'd seen earlier. Too afraid that fire would ignite something in her.

The things Jayden had said, the way she had leaned into her, breathed on her, and whispered in her ear. It had stirred things in her. Things she didn't know she had, much less that needed stirring. Gooseflesh broke out on her arms again and she hugged Lula close, hoping no one would notice. Could Jayden really be interested in her? Or was it some sort of game she was playing with Mel? Kassandra didn't know, but one thing was for certain. She didn't want to be the pawn in anyone's game, no matter how much their presence had stirred her.

"Ms. H, Brandon works here, too," Billy said.

"Really?" She hadn't seen him in years either. "That's great. How's he doing?"

Billy shrugged. "He's okay. Got busted for B&E a while back, but Beaumont saved his ass."

Jayden cleared her throat. "Language."

"Sorry," Billy said. "I still cuss. Can't help it."

"Billy, why don't you get Ms. Haden the information on microchipping?"

Kassandra straightened. "Yes, please do. Lula needs it."

Jayden leaned forward to type on her computer. "It's twenty-five if we do it here. The vet will charge you more."

"Okay, let's go ahead and do it."

Jayden handed over a leash for Lula and a clipboard with a form for her to fill out.

Kassandra clipped on the leash, placed Lula on the floor, and filled out the form. Billy returned with a folder full of information on the microchipping. Kassandra read it over as Jayden entered her info into the computer.

"You've really made an impression on these boys," Jayden said as she typed.

Kassandra met her gaze but only briefly. "They mean a lot to me."

"And you to them. Are you a teacher?"

Kassandra pressed her lips together. Jayden was making a gentle attempt to get to know her. She wasn't sure how she felt about that. "I'm a librarian."

"Oh." Jayden looked at her. "That sounds like a nice, peaceful job."

"Sometimes. Honestly, sometimes it's a little too quiet."

"I can't imagine these guys being quiet."

"They weren't. They kept me company, though."

Jayden looked thoughtful. "I can remember middle school. I was a complete hellion at that age." She smiled and then refocused on the computer.

Kassandra sat quietly, scratching behind Lula's ears. She thought again of Jayden in the warehouse. The things she'd said and the way she'd said them. No one had ever spoken to her like that before. Not even her ex-husband. And he certainly hadn't stirred her like that. Like a flamethrower had gone off just beneath her skin and even beneath her center. She still felt it now, like some sort of throbbing.

She cleared her throat, worried that Jayden could somehow read her thoughts.

She crossed her legs, but it only made the throbbing worse. Jayden pushed an errant strand of dark hair from her piercing gray eyes, and Kassandra reacted to it involuntarily. Her breath caught, and she found herself staring at her long, lean fingers. They were tanned from outdoor work, and she wondered what they felt like when they lightly caressed skin.

"Ms. Haden?"

Kassandra blinked and then warmed. Jayden had been speaking to her. "Yes?"

"Billy's going to take her back now. For the microchip."

"Oh, right." She handed Billy the leash and watched as he knelt and scooped her up gently.

"It won't take long."

Kassandra dug in her small purse for her checkbook. "Do you have a pen?"

Jayden handed her one. Kassandra filled out the check, tore it off, and slid it across the desk. Jayden eyed it and looked at her. "This is really nice of you."

Kassandra held up a hand. "Just please take it. You took care of my dog, and for that I can't thank you enough."

"She freaking rescued her, Ms. H.," Gus said, sitting down next to her. "Beaumont is a badass." He looked to Jayden, who gave him a look. "Sorry. But she like really crawled in and rescued her. I was there with Mel, and even I wouldn't go in that pipe."

Kassandra looked from Gus to Jayden. "Is that true?" Had Jayden been the one to save Lula?

"Hell yes, it's true," Gus said. "Your dog's like stuck in this pipe, right? The sun is setting and we can't see. And we can't figure out why she isn't coming out on her own. So Beaumont, who doesn't wait for the fire department to cut the pipe, says she'll go in. She takes a flashlight and crawls in this tiny space. And it's like muddy and gross and stuff, and she gets in there and she can just barely reach her, right? But she sees that your dog's tag is stuck in this little hole, so she can't move. So Beaumont takes off her collar and backs out with your dog. All like superwoman and shit."

Kassandra stared at him, astonished. She could feel the pulse jump in her neck. She knew she had to look at Jayden, but she didn't want to. She was afraid every emotion she was having would be written all over her face.

"He exaggerates," Jayden said, breaking the silence.

"Like hell I do." Gus looked at Kassandra. "She saved your dog, Ms. H. She saves dogs all the time."

Kassandra looked at Jayden and tried to say thank you. But her voice caved and she had to clear her throat. "Thank you," she finally managed to say.

Jayden's gaze seemed to penetrate right through her. "You're welcome."

Kassandra looked away. Her heart raced and she tried to clear her mind of Jayden's full lips and how she could recall that they'd been inches from her own.

"You know what, Ms. H.?" Gus said. "You should totally volunteer here."

Kassandra jerked her head up. "What?"

"You should. I mean, you love dogs and we love dogs, and Beaumont always needs good volunteers. That way I can see you."

Kassandra rubbed her sweaty palms on her shorts. "I

don't know, Gus." It was difficult enough being around Jayden after what had happened, but now that she knew she'd single-handedly saved her dog, she wondered how much more intense her feelings could get.

"It's true," Jayden said. "I could use another good volunteer. Not just with the dogs, but to help with the teens too."

Kassandra shook her head. She couldn't. No way. Not with Jayden and the way she was feeling. It was too intense and too confusing. What the hell did it mean? Why was it happening?

"I don't know."

Gus placed a hand on her shoulder. "Please? Billy and me, we'll be the best teen staff here. And we'll show you the ropes and help you out."

Kassandra didn't say anything; she just squeezed his hand.

"Well, promise us you will at least think about it," Jayden said.

Billy returned with Lula, and Kassandra held her close. She inhaled the shampoo smell of her fur and closed her eyes for a moment. Right now, she just needed to get out of there. She needed to go home with Lula and put things back together. Then and only then would she tackle Jayden Beaumont.

"I'll think about it," she said, rising to leave. She gave the boys both hugs good-bye and she politely waved to Jayden. She thanked her again and headed for the door. When she stepped through, she took a deep breath and tried to relax. But the heat did little to relax her. She climbed in her car, cranked the air, and sat for a moment. She looked to Lula, who was in the back. Soon the laughter turned to tears, and she found that funny, so she laughed some more. She was having a complete emotional breakdown in her car.

"I'm going crazy, Lula. I'm going insane."

She wiped her eyes and put her car in reverse. And as she pulled out of the parking lot, she heard Jayden's Beaumont's voice in her mind.

I want to read the book of your life. From page one to infinity.

Chapter Six

S o tell me again what happened? Somehow I screwed you?"
Mel asked, taking a sip of her beer.

"Yes, you totally fucked me," Jayden said, finishing her own beer. She motioned for the waitress to bring her another. They were taking a break for dinner at Gina's Bar and Grill, the place they liked to frequent when they had time. Gina's was lesbian owned and most of the clientele was gay, so Mel liked to go there to pick up women. "I came on to her, Mel. Like full on. I almost kissed her."

"Holy shit." Mel grinned. "You're an idiot."

"It's your fault. I thought she was one of yours."

"Oh, no, you don't get to blame this on me. This is all you, Beaumont."

"Bullshit. You're always sending them my way, telling them to flirt with me—"

"Did she flirt with you?"

Jayden hesitated. "Well, no. But—"

"Did she do or say anything to lead you on?"

Jayden laughed a little and squirmed. She didn't like being pinned to a wall. "No."

"Jesus, Beaumont. You hit on a woman just walking in to get her dog? Poor thing must've been scared to death."

"That's just it…she didn't stop me. I mean eventually she did. But for a few seconds, I think she might have…liked it."

"Whoa, hold up. What makes you think that?" She tore off a piece of soft pretzel and dipped it in cheese.

"She responded. I could feel it. Her breathing changed and she shuddered."

"Yeah, probably with fright. A five-foot-ten lesbian was putting the moves on her. She was probably shitting herself."

"Are you done? I'm being serious here."

"So am I. You better hope she doesn't send some maniac after you."

"Oh, my God, knock it off. If I want drama, I'll talk to my teens, thank you very much."

"No, for real. Some of these straight women get really freaked out."

"We're not talking about the ones you hit on."

"Right, we're talking about the one you hit on."

Jayden rolled her eyes and drank her beer. "I don't care what you say. I know she felt something."

Mel pushed the remainder of the pretzel her way. They'd both ordered grilled chicken salads, but they were staving off hunger with the soft pretzels as an appetizer.

"So how did you leave things?" she asked.

Jayden waited until she was finished chewing. "I sort of asked her to volunteer."

"You did what?"

Jayden shrugged. "Gus actually suggested it. I just agreed."

"Wait a minute. Gus?"

"She knows some of the boys. She's a librarian at the middle school they attended."

Mel slapped the table and bit her lower lip mischievously. "You're telling me you hit on a straight librarian?"

"I'm not sure she's straight."

"Oh, this is good, Beaumont. This is so good. You've done crazy things before, but this one. This one might actually take the cake."

"Stop it."

"So you cold hit on her, almost kiss her, and then ask her to come back for more? Are you crazy?"

Jayden tore off another piece of pretzel. "You know, you might be right. I should probably call her to apologize and to reassure her that it won't happen again."

"Have you lost your mind here? No, you do not need to call her. You need to leave her alone."

"She might not come back if I don't call." And Jayden really wanted her to come back.

"Right. And that's a good thing. You want her to forget all about this little escapade. Otherwise her husband or boyfriend or God knows who will come banging on your door."

"She's not married," Jayden said, more to herself.

"Do you hear yourself?" Mel paused, smiled at the waitress, and then forked a bite of her chicken salad. "I'm telling you, leave the poor woman alone."

Jayden forked her own bite. "I'm not sure I can."

Mel chewed, swallowed, and then motioned with her head. "See that woman over there?"

Jayden turned slightly and caught sight of a beautiful woman looking their way. "Yes."

"She's staring at you."

"She is not. She's looking at you."

"Oh no, my friend. Her eyes are on you. And I'll prove it." She took a sip from her beer and grinned. "I'll get up and go to the bathroom. If she follows, then she's after me. If not, then you have to get up and go."

"We're having a conversation here, Mel."

"Right, about a straight woman. Boring. I'm going."

"Really, Mel? Don't you get tired of this?"

"Never." She rose and gave a little wave and disappeared around the corner to the restroom. Jayden continued to eat, not really caring if the woman followed her or not.

"Hi."

Jayden looked up as the woman slid into Mel's chair. Jayden stared for a moment, not quite sure if she was annoyed or not. The woman was beautiful, her smile coy and captivating. Though Jayden noticed, she realized her mind jumped right back to Kassandra. The woman who had mesmerized not only her but her teens as well. So much so, she considered asking this woman to leave so she could finish her meal.

"I thought she'd never leave." The woman laughed a little, pushed back her thick raven hair, and smiled. "I'm Nora."

Jayden took her hand but felt nothing but obligation. "Hello."

"Please tell me that isn't your girlfriend." Her full lips were pink and glossy, and her skin was like creamy mocha. She was beautiful, and normally Jayden would be somewhat intrigued.

"She's not, but—"

"You're not looking, right?"

Jayden thought for a moment. She could say yes and Nora would go. And considering how she was feeling about Kassandra Haden, it would probably be wise. She opened her mouth to speak, but Mel interrupted.

"No, she does not have a girlfriend." She grinned and raised an eyebrow at Jayden.

"Oh, well that's good news." Nora rose, showing off her impossibly tight T-shirt and loose hip-hugger jeans. Jayden knew if she sank her hands into her pockets, her underwear would show. A rush of heat shot through her, but not for Nora.

She was imagining Kassandra in a similar pair, the olive skin of her midriff teasing her.

"Let me give you my number." Nora waited for Jayden to retrieve her phone. She did just so she would leave. Nora leaned in and whispered the number in her ear. She smelled like Burberry cologne, and despite thinking of Kassandra, Jayden's pulse reacted. "Call me. Soon." She walked away and Mel took her seat, obviously pleased with herself.

"Told you so." She took a bite and hummed a little, rubbing it in.

"Shut up." Jayden hated it when Mel was right. She always rubbed it in and she never, ever let her live it down.

"You gonna call her?"

Jayden didn't want to answer. She didn't feel like arguing; she just wanted to eat in peace. She didn't dare tell her that what she really wanted to do was to call Kassandra.

"Can we just eat, please?"

"Fine. Yes. Let's eat. By all means."

Jayden ate her salad and pushed the remainder aside. She never took it with her because they usually got a call and the food often spoiled. She drank her water and mulled over how she was going to get Kassandra to come back. She just had to see her again. But more importantly, she had to talk to her, to apologize, to throw herself at her mercy. She had to do all this without sounding like a creepy stalker.

"By the way," Mel said, having finished her meal as well, "there might be another woman coming by."

"Excuse me?"

"You know, the one I was trying to tell you about today?"

Jayden scowled. "Yeah, the conversation that got me in trouble. Somehow I remember it."

"She's interested in meeting you."

"Mel, no, really. Tell her no. Tell her I'm seeing someone."

"Can't. She's already sold on ya. Said she would come by sometime soon."

"Then I guess I'll have to make sure I'm unavailable."

Mel tipped her beer at her. "Suit yourself."

"No more women, Mel. I mean it."

"Okay, okay."

"Swear it."

"I swear."

"Swear it on the Chili Peppers."

The Red Hot Chili Peppers were their favorite band as teens. They'd been swearing on them for years.

"I swear on the Chili Peppers."

Jayden sighed, knowing that swear was sacred. She sipped again at her water as a call came in. Another dog in danger. They leafed out cash for their meals and rose to leave. As they headed for the truck, Jayden hoped that this would be their last call of the evening, because all she could think about was calling Kassandra.

CHAPTER SEVEN

*J*esus, you're right on. How did she find you? Where did she find you? I want to know so I can go there all the time.

Kassandra tossed and turned, but the words kept replaying in her mind, along with the look of sheer desire that Jayden Beaumont had given her. Her skin came alive again, and the throbbing in her center was back. She squeezed her legs together, hoping that would help, but it only intensified.

What did this mean? What was happening to her body? How could words alone do this to her?

Scott had said many things to her to try to turn her on, but she'd never reacted really at all. And certainly never like this.

She turned and hugged her pillow close. Things with Scott had never been passionate or even very intimate. Sex had been an obligation and she'd never found it pleasurable. His hands had been rough and clumsy, and he had always done the exact same thing time and time again. Kiss the left boob, kiss the right boob, then intercourse. She'd lain there until he finished, which never took very long, but still, she could've done without the whole thing.

So why was she reacting now? And why with Jayden Beaumont? She blinked into the night and recalled Jayden's strong jawline, prominent cheekbones, and mysterious eyes. She thought of her black-as-night hair and the way it fell into her eyes, causing her to run her hands through it. There was something about her that made her want to stare. Her coloration, the contrast, her bone structure, she wasn't sure. She just knew she looked...androgynous. Yes, that was it. She looked androgynous.

Kassandra sat up, heart racing. The realization had stirred her all over again. Why was she so...excited? She flopped back onto the bed and stared at the ceiling. Light filtered in through her locked bedroom door. She'd left the two lamps on in the living room and had placed alarms on all three of her doors. If anyone opened them from the outside, the alarms would beep loudly, waking her and hopefully scaring off any intruder. Even with all that in place, she still didn't feel safe.

She reached down beside the mattress and felt for the hilt of the knife she'd placed there. She knew it was only a pacifier, but having it there made her feel a little better. A gun was out of the question, so the knife was the only option. Whoever had broken into her home had gone through everything, and she felt violated and vulnerable. Knowing someone else had touched her clothing, her jewelry, her possessions...it creeped her out, and now she felt like this person knew her. Knew all about her. Knew that she lived alone. And though she wasn't sure, she suspected that some of her intimates were missing. Panties, bras. It made her panic to think about it. Should she tell the police? Or would they think her paranoid?

Lula stood and walked to her, as if she could sense her growing anxiety. She gave her kisses on the chin and settled down next to her. Kassandra wished she had someone there lying next to her. Not Scott or any other man she knew, but someone else. Someone like—

The phone rang from the night table.

Kassandra reached for it, thinking it might be Katelynn or

Wendy. She hadn't yet called them, too confused about Jayden to know what to say.

"Hello?"

"Hello, is this Ms. Haden?"

Kassandra knitted her brow, concerned. "Yes."

"Hi, it's Jayden Beaumont."

Kassandra sat up again and palmed her chest. "Jayden, yes, hello."

"Am I calling too late?"

"No, no. I, um, was just reading." She went to bed earlier than most, and for some reason she was embarrassed to admit that to Jayden.

"I would've called earlier, but we had a couple of rescue calls." There was a pause, and Kassandra found herself struggling for words.

"Anyway, I just wanted to call and apologize again for what happened today. I—there's no excuse, at least not one that will make sense, and I want you to know I'm not like that. I mean, I wouldn't just come on to you like that. I mean—it won't happen again."

Kassandra's heart fell a little in her chest. "It won't?" Why was she disappointed? Did Jayden not mean all the things she'd said? What exactly had happened? And why was she still reacting to this woman?

"No, it absolutely won't. I need you to know that because I'd really like it if you came to work with us."

Kassandra's mind spun. She wasn't sure what to think or what to feel. At the moment, she felt offended and let down. As if she had indeed been a pawn in some game. Yet she also felt a little thrilled at being wanted.

"I don't know what to say."

"Say yes."

Kassandra couldn't help but smile. "What exactly would I be doing?"

"Well, you would be helping with the dogs, playing with them, socializing them. I need a good people person to interact with families. But mostly, I need someone who's good with the teens. I have ten who currently work with me, and to be honest, I can't spend the time I need to with them. These kids are all in some sort of legal trouble. Graffiti, auto theft, truancy, gangs, breaking and entering. I don't take violent offenders and I don't tolerate drug use, so you don't have to worry about that. Their parole is conditional, meaning they have to work with me so many hours a week in order to remain out of juvie. Many of them need counseling and lots of one-on-one attention. I do my best to guide them through hard work and perseverance, but I don't have the sensitive touch that you seem to have. Bottom line, these kids need people who care about them. And from what I saw today, I'd say you definitely do."

Kassandra felt her mouth open. "I, wow, okay."

"You'll do it?"

"I'll give it a shot."

"Great. Thank you. The boys will be thrilled. I can't wait to tell them."

"When should I come by?"

"Whenever you're free. The teens work weekends and after school on the weekdays."

"Okay, I would come tomorrow, but I'm still putting my house back together after the break-in."

"That's right. I was so sorry to hear that happened to you. Are you okay?"

Kassandra laughed a little. "Physically, I'm fine, yes. And most things are replaceable. But I still feel..."

"Violated?"

"Yes. I don't feel safe."

There was a pause before Jayden spoke. "I've got a great German shepherd mix who'd love to protect you. He gets along great with little dogs."

"Thanks, but Lula likes being the queen of her castle."

Jayden laughed as if she knew the type. "Let me know if you change your mind. Dax is wonderful, so I'd be happy to let him come stay with you for a while. At least until you feel safe."

Kassandra lay back and relaxed a little. It was nice to know that someone other than Katelynn and Wendy cared. "I'll talk to Lula about it."

"I'm sure she'll say yes."

There was another pause and Kassandra wished she could talk to her all night long.

"I should probably let you go."

Again, Kassandra's heart fell. "Okay."

"Have a nice night. I look forward to working with you."

"Thanks, you have a nice night as well."

Kassandra ended the call and placed the phone on her chest. She hugged her pillow and closed her eyes and dreamt of what it would be like to have Jayden Beaumont lying next to her at night.

CHAPTER EIGHT

Jayden stared at her phone after hanging up with Kassandra. She turned up the television and put her bare feet on the ottoman. The conversation had gone better than she'd expected, and she was thrilled that Kassandra was coming back. But her heart ached a little at hearing Kassandra say she was scared. Every fiber in her being wanted to tell Kassandra that she could call her anytime, day or night if she needed to, but Jayden had held back. She had to put a distance between them now and be professional.

Kassandra was not a flirting lesbian; she wasn't one of Mel's relentless girls. Jayden rolled her eyes and sipped her beer. Mel meant well, but lately it was getting old. Mel didn't like her to be alone and she worried about her, Jayden knew that. But she was going to have to find a different way to do things.

Jayden thought of blind dates and she shuddered. No way. Mel would just have to let her handle things. She padded into the kitchen and a few of her dogs followed. She opened the fridge and pulled out the cold lemon water. She'd had her limit for beer, and now she needed to hydrate for tomorrow. She often had to work for hours in the desert heat, and staying hydrated was very important. Most of the time she stuck to water or green tea. Beer, she reserved for slow days only.

She poured herself a glass and returned to the living room. She switched off the television, extinguished the light, and made her way down the hallway. This time all of her dogs followed, and she slowed as she eyed the framed photos on the wall. She stopped and touched the one of her grandmother, Rose. She loved her no end and missed her so much. She'd been the one to take her in after the sudden death of her mother. She'd put up with her through all the trouble she'd caused, loved her, nurtured her, guided her. And then she'd kicked her in the ass, insisting she spend her free time working with abandoned animals. Jayden had fought it at first, not liking her free time being taken away. But rather quickly she found herself growing attached to the animals and concerned about their well-being. Soon she'd spent most of her time at a large ranch, working with the animals and doing chores for the owner. Oftentimes, Grandma Rose had to insist she come home for the evening.

Jayden mouthed *I love you* to the photo and continued on. She smiled at the old photos of her and Mel. They'd met in juvie, when Jayden had been pinched for riding in a stolen car with a friend. She hadn't stolen the car, nor had she known it was stolen, but her so-called friend had told a different story to the police. Jayden couldn't prove her innocence, and having a joint on her hadn't helped. Her prints had been all over the car, and she'd been with her friend most of the day, making stops here and there, giving witnesses an ample view of the both of them driving around in the car.

She sighed as she entered her bedroom and flicked on the light. Though those days were long gone, she still regretted them and the way she'd often behaved. She'd just been so lost with her mother, and after she'd died in the accident, Jayden had acted out, thinking nothing really mattered anymore. She knew what her teens at the shelter were going through and how they were feeling. Many didn't have people that cared like Grandma Rose. Many had already been through more than she could imagine.

She set her drink on the night table, stripped out of her clothes, and crossed to the bathroom. She'd already showered, so she brushed her teeth and returned to the bed. Three of her dogs were already on it, curled up and ready to sleep. The other four were either tucked away in a dog bed or sprawled out on their sides on the floor. She whistled for Dax and scratched his head as she crawled under the covers.

Her mind went to Kassandra and how she wished she could help her. Dax would definitely do the trick. But secretly she wished she could be the solution. She imagined knocking on Kassandra's door, embracing her in a comforting hug, and then walking inside to check the place out to make her feel safer. She'd calm her down, hold her hand. Then she'd gladly stay when Kassandra asked and she'd crawl into bed next to her, hold her, listen to her breathe while she drifted off to sleep. Then, in the morning, before she woke, she'd make breakfast for her.

"That sounds nice, doesn't it, Dax?"

He twitched his ears and licked her wrist.

"We could make her feel safe, couldn't we?"

She reached for her water and turned on her Kindle. She liked to read before bed, but tonight she knew it would be difficult to concentrate. She couldn't stop thinking about the phone call. And she couldn't stop thinking about Kassandra walking into the front office again. Would she exude the same quiet beauty? Would she be shy? Would she look at her differently?

"That's not the big question is it, Dax?" She kissed him back on the nose. "The big question is…can I behave like a normal person and not stare at her. What do you think? Think I can do it?"

She wasn't used to being overly interested in a woman. Usually they came after her, full force. And there had always been plenty to choose from. But one that intrigued her, brought a little mystery…a woman like that had long eluded her. Until now.

She eyed her Kindle and turned it off. She took several sips of water and then extinguished the light. She loved on Cooper, who lay at her side next to Dax. As she settled down next to them, she decided to tell herself her own story. One about Kassandra and herself. It was bound to be a good one.

CHAPTER NINE

Kassandra eyed the digital clock on the wall again. She'd been checking it periodically, then chastising herself for it. She was anxious and excited about going to Angel's Wings after work, and she felt ridiculous. What was the big deal? She'd go and help with the kids. End of story. But as she reshelved the last book for the day, she knew there was more to it. And it had everything to do with Jayden Beaumont.

Her heart fluttered as Jayden's face came to mind. She tried to brush it off while wheeling the book cart behind the counter, but she didn't have much luck. Jayden had been in her mind all day. Did she like her? Had she meant those things she'd said? What did it mean? What should she do?

Suddenly, the double doors opened and Tony burst through. He shrugged off his backpack and slung it against the wall.

"I hate this fucking place and I hate home. I'm not going home."

Kassandra continued to turn off the computers. She didn't speak, knowing he would vent it all out. He was agitated, and the best thing to do was to remain calm and distract him a little while he vented.

"Can you switch off those computers on the far table?"

His body went from rigid and aggressive to calm and relaxed. She'd caught him off guard, forcing him to downshift. He loved helping her in the library, and she played that to her advantage, knowing it helped calm him.

He crossed to the table and began shutting the computers down. "I'm not going home, Ms. H. I'm just not. They can fucking kiss my ass."

"If you're going to help me, you can't use that language," she said softly.

He shook his head, his mind still on his troubles. "They have all these rules. Like they're fu—like they're dictators. You know, like Hitler and shi—stuff."

"Parents have a difficult job. It isn't easy for them."

"Ha! Try my absent mother and asshole uncle. Mom is never home and my uncle is always partying with his messed-up friends. I have to share a room with that di—jerk."

Kassandra felt for him. He often complained about his home life. But he'd never gone into detail.

"Where will you go, if you don't go home?"

He shrugged. "I don't know. Probably my place. I got a place."

Kassandra grew concerned. "Where is it? Is it safe?"

Again, he shrugged. "It has been so far. And I don't tell anyone about my place."

"Why not?"

"Because it's where I go when I don't want to be found."

"What about your brothers and sisters?"

"Man, they're with my abuela. Have been for weeks."

"Can't you go there? I'm sure she'd love to have you."

He made a noise of disgust and sank into a chair. "She hates me. Calls me crazy because of my bipolar. Says all I need is a good beating."

"She hits you?"

"Not anymore. I don't let her. I don't stick around to wait for her to try either."

Kassandra sat across from him. "I have to tell someone if you're really not going to go home."

"Who, that cop? Man, he won't do shit. They won't care until my mom calls me in missing, and if she don't come home, she won't even know."

"Tell me why you don't want to go home?"

He pushed out a breath and shifted as if uncomfortable. "Nothing. It's all good." He stared off in the distance, careful not to meet her gaze.

Kassandra knew she couldn't promise him that she wouldn't tell anyone. If he wasn't being cared for or if he was being abused, she'd have to tell.

"Is someone hurting you?"

He made a face of disgust. "Cha, no. No way. Ain't nobody laying a finger on me."

"Then why?"

He shook his head and looked away again. "Look, I shouldn't have said anything. At least I got a bed and a blanket. Well, sometimes. If my asshole uncle doesn't have one of his friends passed out on my bed."

Kassandra studied him for a moment. He had on a familiar shirt and jeans. The jeans were a bit dirty and so were his sneakers. But she rarely saw a boy who didn't have dirt on his pants and shoes. His skin looked clean, his nails were chewed, along with the skin around them. His hair was buzzed very close to his head. Overall, he looked like an average kid, though she did notice that his face looked a little thinner. Even so, she was going to talk to the counselor about him just to be safe.

Kassandra wanted to give him her number, but there were

rules against that. Teachers had to have boundaries. "Where are you going to go now?"

"I don't know. Probably the dollar cinema."

"You have money?"

"Yeah, I took some off a loser last night. He was passed out in my bathtub."

Kassandra sighed. The situation wasn't good. "Can you wait right here? I need to make a phone call."

He stood, looking alarmed. "Hell no. You're going to call that counselor, aren't you?"

"I'm just trying to get you some help." She held up her palms. "We need to find you a safe place."

"I'm fine. I told you nobody touches me. I shoulda never said anything."

She stood and spoke very softly. "I know, I heard you, okay? But for some reason you don't want to go home, and that concerns me. I'm worried about you."

"Yeah, well, don't bother. Nobody else gives a shit." He retrieved his backpack and shrugged it over his shoulder.

"Please don't go. Stay here with me and we'll call someone and work it out."

"Like who? The counselor? The cops? Man, fuck them. They just see me as some psycho kid who steals. They just wanna pinch me and lock me away."

Kassandra placed a hand gently on his shoulder. "Not everyone is bad. There are good people who can help. People like me."

He met her eyes, burning a pain filled stare into her. "You can't help me, Ms. H. No one can."

He crossed the room and pushed through the doors, leaving Kassandra alone in his wake.

CHAPTER TEN

Jayden looked up for the fifth time that afternoon. There were three new people at the counter, but Kassandra wasn't one of them. Normally, Jayden would be on the grounds, working with dogs or out on a call. But today she'd sent others out because she wanted to be the one to greet Kassandra.

"This is crazy, you know," Mel said, sliding into the chair in front of Jayden's desk.

"What?" Jayden leaned to her left to look around her.

"This madness. You're sitting here waiting for her, aren't you?"

"Maybe. Now go away."

Mel scoffed. "And miss this freak show? No way."

"There's nothing to see. Now beat it."

Mel leaned into her line of sight. "Really? Because it looks like you're nearly peeing your pants while waiting for a woman."

Jayden stood as the front door opened. Kassandra walked in and stood behind the others as if waiting in line.

"Not peeing. Just anticipating. Now get lost." She rounded her desk and walked to the counter. She opened the waist-high door and came to stand in front of Kassandra.

"You made it." Jayden smiled. Kassandra looked beautiful

in the sunlight streaming through the window. Her blond hair shimmered and her skin looked soft and supple. Good enough to touch. Jayden felt herself heat at the thought. "Good to see you."

Kassandra returned the smile and tucked a strand of hair behind her ear. "Thanks. Sorry I'm late. I got held up at school."

"No, you're fine. Whenever you can make it is fine." Jayden didn't mention that she'd been anxiously anticipating her for the last hour. Jumping every time the door opened.

"I actually had some trouble concerning a student." She looked serious. "I was wondering if I could talk to you about it."

Jayden felt honored. "Sure. Come on back."

She led the way to her desk where Mel was sitting with her head craned to stare at them.

Jayden gave her a look and cleared her throat. "Ahem. Don't you have some work to do?" She forced a smile at her as she sat behind her desk and Kassandra sat across from her.

"Oh, right. I have the—you know—thing." She stood and looked to Kassandra. "I'm Mel, by the way."

"Oh, hi. I'm—"

"Kassandra, right." She took her hand and smiled. "I've heard a lot about you."

"You have?" Kassandra looked to Jayden, who wanted to die. She could feel herself slowly sinking in the chair.

"Good things, though," Mel said quickly. "I hear you're going to join us."

Kassandra looked back to Mel, who finally released her hand. "Yes, well, I'm giving it a shot."

"Well, if anyone can convince you to stay, it's Jayden." She gave Jayden a wink. "Nice to meet you," she said, walking away.

Kassandra waved. "Nice to meet you."

Jayden was still burning with embarrassment. She tried a smile and linked her nervous fingers together in her lap.

"So, you were saying?"

But Kassandra looked distant, almost...heartbroken.

"She's the one who played the trick on you, with me?" Her eyes were glossy and yet searing with intensity.

Jayden leaned forward, heart suddenly tripping over itself. "I—"

"No, I don't want to know." She looked at her own hands and then back up. "Just know that I don't intend to be the butt of any jokes. I'm only here because you said it wouldn't happen again."

Jayden opened her mouth, but no words came out. "I-I can assure you it won't. And just so you know, you weren't something we were joking about. It was a misunderstanding."

Kassandra wrung her hands and Jayden felt like an ass. How could she make this right? She would do anything to not see hurt in her eyes.

"I'm really sorry," she said. "I thought you were a woman who had come to meet me." She shook with nerves, but she knew the truth was her last shot. "I—you were really beautiful and I made a fool out of myself." She sighed, wishing like hell she could take back that moment. Get a do-over somehow.

Kassandra sat in silence. When she did speak, her voice had a new strength to it. "You didn't know the woman?"

"No. Mel had just told me she would be stopping by. I saw you and I just assumed it was you." She wanted to say hoped, but she left that out.

"You...like women?"

Jayden reminded herself to breathe. "Yes." It was a bold question and it implied that Kassandra didn't. "I hope that won't be a problem. We have a few gay staff members."

"Oh, right. Of course, No, it's not a problem. I just—I. My friends are lesbians."

Jayden smiled at Kassandra's nervousness. "So, are we okay now?"

Kassandra smiled softly in return. "Yes."

"Good." Jayden rose and walked with her to the kennels. "I think it's best if you meet the dogs first."

Kassandra followed, nodding polite hellos to those that introduced themselves on the way. Jayden liked her calm presence, her humble beauty, and her polite ways. She was a classy woman, very down-to-earth. Jayden wondered again if she had anyone special in her life. Surely she dated. A woman like her was quite a catch. Both men and women were probably all over her.

Like Jayden.

Jayden grimaced at her behavior. But she had to shake it off. Onward and forward. She'd make it up to her. She just didn't know how yet.

They entered the kennels and Jayden introduced her to each and every dog. Kassandra was open and friendly, talking to each one, even insisting on petting them. Jayden watched her closely, moved by her inner beauty. She seemed to radiate love to the dogs, and they seemed to sense it, eating up her ample affection.

When they left the kennels, which was hard to do for Kassandra, Jayden showed her the warehouse and where they stored food and supplies. Then she showed her three grass lots and the hiking path where they often took the dogs for long walks.

"You've got a lot of land here," Kassandra said, shading her brow from the sun.

"I do. I'm lucky. We use almost all of it."

"Who lives there?" Kassandra pointed to Jayden's house.

"I do."

"Oh. Really?"

"Yep. This is all mine. Left to me by my grandmother, Rose."

"Is she the one who started the shelter?"

Jayden started walking slowly toward the house. Kassandra matched her stride. "She was a big supporter. She spent many hours helping out, walking dogs, greeting people. She was an amazing person."

"So, this was your dream?"

"Yes. Since I was sixteen."

"That's really great, you know, seeing your dream come true."

"It is." Jayden noticed that her body language had changed. She was quiet. Almost sad. "What's your dream, Kassandra?"

"Mine? Gosh, no one has ever asked me that before."

"Then you're not hanging out with the right people."

Kassandra laughed. "Nah, my friends are great."

"The lesbians?"

"Yes."

They stopped on the front porch. Kassandra seemed to notice for the first time where they were.

"There's someone else I want you to meet," Jayden said, unlocking the door.

"Okaaay." Kassandra stepped inside after her and closed the door.

Jayden greeted her dogs eagerly, shooing them back so Kassandra could enter. "Excuse their enthusiasm. Guys, calm." She straightened and held up a finger. The dogs at once sat at attention. Eugene, the loving basset, yawned loudly and swung his tail.

"Wow. Very impressive."

"They are, aren't they?" Jayden dug in the pocket of her cargo shorts and broke up small bits of liver treats. She gave each dog a nibble as she praised them. "Guys, this is Kassandra. She's very nice, so I want you to greet her calmly. Got it? Calm."

The dogs wagged their tails but remained sitting. "Dax, come." The German shepherd mix hurried to her, nosing her hands for treats. "Good boy." She gave him a treat and brought him to Kassandra. "Kassandra, this is Dax." Jayden stroked his head and Kassandra bent to pet him.

"He's beautiful," she said, now kneeling to rub him on his neck and shoulders.

"He's a wonderful dog. Very alert, very protective. And he gets along great with these guys."

Kassandra laughed as he kissed her on the mouth. "He's affectionate."

"Oh, yes."

"You want me to take him, don't you?"

Jayden knelt and called her other pups over. She loved on each of them, as did Kassandra. "I don't like hearing that you're afraid. No one should feel that way in their own home."

Kassandra loved on the dogs in silence, paying particular attention to Dax.

"No pressure," Jayden said. "Just wanted you to meet him."

Kassandra smiled. "Thanks," she said softly. She straightened and looked around. "You have a nice home."

Jayden showed her the living room. "Thanks. Grandma liked her space. We always had animals and they always lived inside with us."

"It was your grandmother's?"

"Yes. She lived in this house for fifty-five years." Jayden

walked to the bookshelf and retrieved a photo. She handed it to Kassandra. "That's her when she and my grandpa first moved in. You can see the front porch in the background."

"Wow. She was beautiful."

"She was a looker."

"I can see the resemblance." Kassandra looked at her. "The hair and eyes."

"I used to get that a lot. People used to think I was hers. Might as well have been. I always got along better with her than I did my mother."

Kassandra returned the photo. She looked as if she wanted to ask a question but changed her mind.

"Anyway, that's the story on the house." She placed the photo back on the bookshelf. "Mel and I have remodeled quite a bit over the years."

"I can tell. It's nice."

Jayden scratched Dax on the head. Most of the other dogs had assumed their positions on the floor or couch.

"You like to read," Kassandra said, eyeing the bookshelf.

Jayden turned to follow her line of sight. "I do."

"You like noirs," she said softly.

Jayden smiled. "Guilty."

"So do I."

"If you see anything you like, you're welcome to borrow it."

Kassandra flushed a little. "Thanks, but—"

Jayden held up a hand. "No pressure."

"Okay." She smiled and then looked away bashfully.

Jayden had the feeling that she didn't trust easily. Didn't let people in. She was so guarded, afraid to let others help her.

"I'll keep offering," Jayden said. "But there's never any pressure. I like to help my friends. It's what I do." She offered a smile and eased her hands into her pockets. "Come on, I'll show you the rest of the place."

They said good-bye to the dogs and headed back out into the heat.

CHAPTER ELEVEN

K assandra walked with Jayden around the property. The day
was hot and the sun was bright, so Jayden tried her best to
give a quick tour. The shelter, along with Jayden's house, sat
on seven acres. Horse property surrounded Jayden's, and the
area seemed very quiet and peaceful. People just wanting to
care for their animals north of the city.

Kassandra wondered if she could see the stars at night out
there. She'd have to ask Jayden sometime. Kassandra loved
the night sky. It reminded her of childhood trips to Baja. She'd
sit out by the soothing sound of the ocean and stare up at the
millions of stars. It had been the most beautiful thing she'd
seen to date.

"Something on your mind?" Jayden asked as they headed
for the front office once again.

"It's a nice place," she said. And it was. The grounds
were nice, well kept. The trees were large and provided much-
needed shade. She even had wildflowers growing in some
areas. "You've done a good job."

"Thanks. That's always nice to hear."

Kassandra wanted to ask her about books, the stars, her
dogs, her home, but she didn't dare. She was afraid of her
interest and more afraid of the answers. What if Jayden was
intelligent, funny, sensitive, and caring? It was already looking

like she was. And that only intrigued her more. Which scared the hell out of her.

"You can ask me anything you want," Jayden said just before they entered.

She seemed to be reading her mind, and Kassandra panicked, hoping her interest wasn't written all over her face.

"Okay." She tried to smile, but she knew it wasn't relaxed. So she looked away as they entered the air-conditioned office. She breathed in deeply and followed Jayden to her desk. The air felt good, instantly cooling the sweat on her skin. She sank into a chair and tried not to stare at the gleam of sweat on Jayden's tanned skin. Her high cheekbones had been kissed by the sun, causing them to slightly redden. Yet her gray eyes remained cool, like tempting pools in a landscape of hot desert.

"Here you go." Jayden retrieved two bottles of cold water from the mini fridge behind her desk. She handed one to Kassandra.

"Thank you." Kassandra opened it at once and drank.

"We keep cold water everywhere. In that fridge in the warehouse, in here, and in the old vending machines throughout the property. You don't have to have change. Just push the button."

Kassandra nodded, recalling now that Jayden had said something about them earlier.

"Please make sure you stay hydrated. It's the number one rule while working here in the heat. Now," she said while digging through her file cabinet, "it would probably help you to read over these files on the kids."

She set a stack in front of her. "It helps to know their history and home life. I had to fight for most of that information. The kids, they don't like talking about home."

"I seem to be finding that out," Kassandra said, thinking of Tony.

"Most of it I found out on my own. The kids trust me, for the most part."

"I can see why. You really care." Kassandra knew it wasn't easy getting personal information from teenagers. It must've taken Jayden quite a while to get that much information.

"These ten are lucky. They still have guardians who care. Those that don't...they don't tend to last very long here."

"It's all about the home life," Kassandra said.

"That's why I treat these kids like family. To me they are. To the dogs they are."

"I understand." She wished she could do more for her students at school. "I have a student, one who doesn't like going home."

"That doesn't sound good," Jayden said. "Has he told you why?"

"Bits and pieces. It sounds like the mother is mostly gone and the uncle has parties where people pass out all over the house, including the boy's bed."

"Oh, geez." Jayden dug through a Rolodex. "Do you think he's neglected?"

"That's just it, I don't know what to think. He looks clean and groomed, and though he's lost weight lately, he looks like he eats. What really concerns me is he says he doesn't go home sometimes. He has a secret place he goes to, and worse yet, no one at home notices when he's gone."

Jayden plucked a card from her Rolodex and began copying the information on a notepad. Then she fingered through other cards and did the same.

"Do you know anything else? Is there another family member you can contact?"

"No. I've spoken to the counselor before about him, and she said she'd look into things, but I don't feel like she really gets it. She doesn't know Tony like I do. He clammed up when I told him I was going to speak to her."

Jayden tore off the piece of paper she'd written on and handed it over. "Sounds like he's afraid he'll get put into the system. Like maybe he's been there before."

Kassandra eyed the paper. "He said something about being locked up."

Jayden pointed to the paper. "Those are numbers to hotlines, help lines, and addresses to shelters. The last number is for my friend at Child Protective Services. Give him a call. He's probably going to suggest that you file a report. They'll investigate."

"You're right. I think this is what he's afraid of. He'll be so upset."

"But he'll be alive. He'll be fed with a warm bed."

"Will he? God, I just really don't want to let him down. He feels like nobody cares."

Jayden met her gaze. "The best thing you can do for him is to listen, be there for him, and call my friend. I know it isn't easy. These kids, they all think they can handle it on their own. But they need help." Jayden's voice softened. "I've had to make several of these calls, and each time it tore my heart out. But letting it go…no way. The streets, they're no place for a kid. If he's sleeping on the streets or an abandoned place, think of the danger he's in. I had a kid once, she was running away after school and sleeping in a motel. Wasn't long before a pimp found her and had her turning tricks for him just to earn her bed at night."

"Oh, my God."

"When I found out, which wasn't easy to do, by the way, I made the call and she got put in the system. She hated me at first, but she comes to visit now. She's doing okay."

Kassandra pushed out a long breath. "Thanks." She held up the paper before folding it and putting it in her purse.

"In the meantime, if you want to help him, bring him a bag of food every day. Enough for three meals. Give him those numbers and addresses. Give him change for the pay phones. And tell him you care and you'll be there for him."

Kassandra nodded. "Okay."

"If you ever have questions or just need an ear, you can call me. Sometimes dealing with this stuff…it's heart wrenching."

Kassandra felt her heart warm. "Thank you."

"He's lucky he has you."

The front doors chimed behind Kassandra. Jayden looked up and smiled, and Kassandra turned to see a young boy with blond hair jumping up and down in front of the counter.

"Jayden, I'm here. I'm here!"

Jayden rounded her desk and Kassandra watched as she walked to the counter, swung open the door, and let him through. He threw his arms around her, obviously catching her by surprise.

"Whoa there, guy. Take it easy or you're going to squeeze me to death." Jayden smiled at Kassandra. "Where's your mom?"

The boy released his grip and looked up at her. "Mom said she'd be back at six. She's going to run some errands."

A staff member, a woman who had Allie on her name tag, spoke up from behind her desk. "Yeah, she called. I told her it was fine."

Jayden gave her a look. "You didn't tell me."

Allie pointed without looking up. "It's in your message pile that you never look at."

Jayden placed her hand on the boy's shoulder. "Kassandra, this is John. He's going to be helping me out today."

The boy stuck out his hand. Impressed, Kassandra smiled and shook it. "Nice to meet you, John."

"Nice to meet you, ma'am."

"Where did you learn to shake hands like that?" Jayden asked.

"My dad." He grinned. "He said it's important."

"It is," Kassandra said. "You did a very good job."

He sat on the chair next to her and swung his knobby legs. "I'm here to work with Cooper." He tugged on the bill of his Arizona Cardinals ball cap. "Who do you work with?"

"I think I'm here to work with the kids."

"Like me?"

Kassandra laughed a little at his eagerness. "Maybe."

"Cool! And you can meet Cooper. He's gonna be my dog if Jayden fixes him."

"He is?"

"Yeah. That's why I'm here. I'm gonna help her fix him."

Jayden stood in a relaxed position with her arms crossed over her chest. She was smiling, obviously enjoying the exchange.

"What do you say, bud? You ready to get started?" she asked.

He stood at once. "Yep."

Jayden wrapped her arm around his shoulder and led him toward the warehouse door. "You'll be okay for a while?" she asked Kassandra.

"Yes." Kassandra held up a file, knowing she had a lot of reading to do.

"Some of the teens are already here. I'll send some your way when I see them." She disappeared through the door with John who was already chatting away.

Kassandra relaxed, drank her water, and dug into the files.

Most of the kids sounded a lot like the students that attended her school. Small crimes, truancy, school suspensions, running away. She knew the stories all too well. But Jayden had been right. All ten of the kids seemed to have one or more guardians that still cared. By the look of the notes, it seemed that Jayden had good communication with the guardians. She spoke to them regularly, checking in on the kids to see how they were doing at home and school. She was also in contact with the probation officers.

Kassandra was impressed. Jayden really did care about these kids. She had birthdays highlighted, favorite foods, colors, and hobbies noted. And she took great care in placing certain kids with certain dogs. And all the kids had gone through hours of training.

She closed one of the last files as Billy and Gus walked in all grins. "Ms. H.!"

"You're here!"

Gus embraced her, followed by Billy. Both the boys had a bottle of Coke in their hands, and Gus was smacking on gum. Both wore the green polo shirts with the shelter's emblem on the breast. And both had on khaki shorts, though they were worn lower than the other staff's. Gus had on yellow work boots, and Billy had on high-top sneakers. Their shoes were covered in dust and their skin glistened with sweat.

"I see you guys have been working hard."

"Can you smell us?" Gus asked playfully. "Because Billy stinks."

"Shut up, fool, I do not."

She pointed at the Cokes. "Where did you get those?"

"The fridge in the warehouse," Billy said, taking a swig.

"We hide them in the drawers under Beaumont's bottles of green tea."

"Yeah, we need something normal every once in a while. Other than water and that tea stuff she drinks."

"We got chocolate hidden, too," Billy said. "But don't tell. Beaumont doesn't like sugar. She's like a health freak."

Kassandra held up her fingers. "Scout's honor."

"Come on, we'll take you to the new intakes and show you what we do."

Gus led the way, followed by Billy. They both stopped at the door, downed their Cokes, and then hid them in the trash bin.

"She must be really serious about the sugar," Kassandra said.

"You have no idea," Gus said, smiling.

They pushed through the door and entered the warehouse. It was less stuffy than it had been before, and Kassandra noted large fans in the corners. But what she really focused on was Jayden, in the center of the floor space, kneeling with a dog. John was about twenty feet away, intently focused on the dog. She watched as he called the dog, encouraging him by patting his knee. The dog, who was called Cooper, hesitated at first, but with Jayden's gentle persuading, he eventually walked slowly up to the boy and took the treat.

John praised him well, but he didn't get overexcited. He remained very calm, scratching Cooper on the chin. Jayden approached, all smiles. She high-fived him and knelt to praise Cooper. Then she had John kneel and give Cooper another treat and she took his hand and helped him stroke the shy dog. She spoke softly to him as they stroked Cooper, words Kassandra could not hear. But the scene was touching, and Kassandra found herself heating like she had when she'd stared at Jayden's eyes and sweat slicked skin.

She looked away, afraid someone would see her staring.

But Gus and Billy were over at the supplies, sifting through collars and grabbing two light leashes. When they caught sight of her, they motioned for her to follow them into the private medical room, the place where they had kept Lula. She entered a little warily, still remembering the emotion that had overcome her when she'd first held Lula after her ordeal. It had been a moment she'd never forget.

"We've got two new ones today," Billy said, setting the leashes on the table. He moved to the stainless steel kennels where two small dogs were lying on soft blankets. One dog, a small brown Chihuahua, was jumping at the door and barking, tail wagging. The other dog, a white poodle mix, was cowering in the corner.

Kassandra's heart surged at the sight and she had a longing to hold the scared one and comfort it. "Where are they from?"

Gus took the clipboard off the door of the white one. "This is Cookie. She was given up because her family had to move into a place that didn't allow dogs. She's three years old, spayed, vaccines current. But she's afraid. Says here she's afraid of everything. People, leashes, dog toys. Says she was around toddlers who tried to carry her often. So she would do best around adults. Temperament is good. No food aggression." He looked at her and rehung the clipboard. "Poor girl." He pulled on latex gloves and tossed some to Kassandra. "I'm going to get her out," he said to Gus, who was also putting on gloves.

"All right, bro, I'll take no-name here." He paused to read the clipboard. "This little guy is young. Less than a year old. Found in a home with ten other Chihuahuas. Owner was a breeder, couldn't handle them all anymore."

"He has no name?" Kassandra asked.

"Nah. Says the owner had no names for them. She was still trying to sell them." Gus opened the door and took the little dog in his arms. He spoke softly to him and held him close. "He looks like a Juan," he said with a smile. "Yeah, a Juan Pablo. That's what his name will be." He held him up and the dog tried to lick his face. Gus laughed. "I think he likes it."

He placed him on the table and got busy slipping on a collar, while Billy carefully picked up Cookie, the anxious poodle mix. He cooed to her and held her close. Kassandra could tell she was trembling.

"It's okay, mija," Billy said to her. "No one will hurt you here." He, too, placed her on the table and collared and leashed her. When they were ready they lifted the dogs again and headed out the door, crossing to the back warehouse doors. The grass lots sat just outside the doors. The boys carried the dogs to two separate lots, where they stepped inside and closed the gates. Billy encouraged Kassandra to follow him inside with Cookie.

He set her down on the grass, and she cowered near his feet. Kassandra knelt and spoke softly to her, trying to get her to come to her. But Cookie merely whined and lay on the grass.

"This will help a lot." Billy gave her a handful of treats.

Kassandra placed her hand palm up a few inches from her and called her name. Cookie came to her slowly and took the treat. Kassandra praised her and stroked her lightly. Cookie rolled onto her back and Billy laughed.

"That's what she's after. A belly rub."

"Can you blame her?" Kassandra lightly stroked her belly, and when she hit a certain spot Cookie's leg kicked.

Kassandra smiled and sat on the grass. She placed all but a few treats in her pocket. She held one out and called for the dog. Cookie tilted her head as her name was called and then cautiously approached. When she took the treat, Kassandra praised her again.

Billy unhooked her leash and sat down next to Kassandra,

treats in hand. As Cookie grew braver, she took more treats and accepted more pats of affection, and then she began exploring the grass.

"I like working with dogs like this," Billy said, leaning back on his hands. "You know, the ones who are afraid. It's amazing to me how, with a little love, they change."

"The same can be said for you," Kassandra said, recalling his file. "You seem to be doing really well, Billy."

He shrugged and grinned slyly as if he were proud, yet embarrassed. "Yeah, you know. I do all right."

"How's school?"

"It's okay, I guess. I mean, I'm so bored most of the time. But I really like art. It's my favorite class. Right now, we're doing abstract and I'm really good at it."

"That's great." She'd read that while his grades weren't great, he did seem to excel in areas where he was hands-on. Classes like art and guitar, he seemed to thrive in. "I take it you still draw?"

"Yeah. I love it. I do it mostly at home, though. You know, when my pop's watching TV and it's boring. I just spread out on the floor and draw."

"Will you bring me some so I can see? I always liked looking at your artwork."

He smiled. "Sure, yeah. I'll even drive you around, show you some of my tags."

Kassandra shoved him playfully. "Very funny."

"Hey, you know, some of them I'm proud of."

"We won't be doing that," she said. He'd been busted a few times too many for graffiti.

He stared off into the sun, and Cookie continued to explore the lot, relieving herself and sniffing around. Someone drove by in a golf cart, and the boys whistled a salute while to their right, Jayden emerged with John walking Cooper. They waved and crossed to the far lot, where they entered and began playing fetch.

Kassandra watched them from afar, her heart pounding at the way Jayden moved, so strong and sure of herself.

"Beaumont's tough, but she's a nice lady," Billy said, following her line of sight.

Kassandra tore her eyes away, embarrassed at having been caught staring. "She seems very nice."

"She's helped me out big-time."

Kassandra smiled. "I'm glad."

"Next to you, she's like my favorite adult." He stood, brushed himself off, and offered Kassandra a hand.

She gladly took it and stood, the heat finally seeping into her bones. It was time to head back indoors. Cookie was panting but seemingly happy. Billy scooped her up.

"Bath time, little one," he said.

Kassandra glanced over at Jayden again. She was kneeling next to the boy, talking with him intently. While she wanted nothing more than to go inside and help Billy and Gus bathe the new dogs, a small but growing part of her wanted to stay and stare at Jayden.

"You coming, Ms. H?" Gus asked, following Billy to the door.

Kassandra tore her eyes away from Jayden. Her interest in Jayden would have to be her little secret. And right now, she knew all she had to focus on was getting better at hiding it.

CHAPTER TWELVE

Jayden sang to the dogs in the kennel, belting out morning Sinatra. The dawn was fresh and even a little cool, September a nice welcome from the dreaded summer heat they'd just suffered through. The dogs howled and did spinning dances, anxious to get outside and run in the fresh air. She opened kennel after kennel and leashed ten dogs, based on excitement level and temperament. Then she exited out the back and trotted with them to the fenced lots. Faith stood by at the first one and helped her release each dog to run free. Then they stepped back, watched the gray light turn to a faded gold, and smiled as the dogs ran and played.

Faith sipped coffee from a large travel mug. She'd always been a caffeine junkie. It was the one vice she couldn't give up. She was in her early twenties and had been with Jayden since she was fifteen after a fresh stint in juvie for damaging property and running away from a foster home. The truth, however, was that her foster parent was abusing her and she'd lost her temper and taken a bat to his belongings. He called the police and she ran. It had taken Jayden over a year to get the truth from her. That's how much fear she had of him.

Faith slurped. "News people here yet?"

Jayden glanced at her watch. "Soon."

"You nervous?"

"We've done interviews before." She knelt and rubbed a boxer furiously. He ran off, tail tucked with excitement, and scooted around the grassy lot.

"I am," Faith said. She looked at her, waiting for her reaction. "What?"

She laughed. "Faith, there is no need for you to be nervous. You've got movie star looks. And besides, it's about the dogs. Just focus on showing them off."

"Well, we can't all be cool like you, Beaumont."

She nudged her and knelt to throw a ball for a couple of hopping dogs. They were clean and brushed, ready for some much-needed attention. Allie had even tied on her homemade bandannas for an added touch. Jayden waved at her as she opened the second lot, a cluster of eager dogs tugging on her. Jayden left Faith to help her. They released the dogs and watched them run and bark, tearing up clumps of grass.

"They sure love this weather," Allie said, rubbing her eyes and then yawning. It was rare to see her act so…human.

"I do too," Jayden said, wrapping an arm around her for a quick squeeze. "If you were awake, I think you'd like it, too."

Allie laughed. "Shut up. You know mornings aren't my thing."

"Want some coffee? Faith always makes some first thing."

"Is it decaf?"

"Maybe." Jayden tried to avoid caffeine. She'd stopped drinking it in her teens after juvie. A counselor had suggested it, and she couldn't believe the change in her anxiety and mood.

"Then what's the point, Beaumont?"

"It's still coffee," Jayden said as she walked away. "Besides, I know you all have a stash of caffeinated somewhere. Just ask her." She headed out of the lot and crossed to the office. Her staff had arrived earlier than usual to prepare for the news crew. She could hear them chatting excitedly, moving around to set things up before she entered the office.

"Good morning, everyone," she said as she entered.

They looked up and groaned back at her.

"Glad everyone is up and at 'em."

The office looked impeccable. Papers were filed, desks dusted, industrial carpet vacuumed. She even smelled vanilla. Someone had candles burning. "This place looks great," she said, walking to the walls to check out the new framed photographs.

"These are fantastic." One of their volunteers was into photography, and she often took photos of families with their adopted pets. They used them for social media and local ads. But now they were framed and hanging on the walls of the office. Jayden couldn't believe how cozy and welcoming it made the place feel.

Jayden got a little choked up, so thankful for her friends and staff. They were family, and to her, family was everything. She cleared her throat.

"If I could have everyone's attention, please."

The room grew quiet, and a small mass of green polos stood at attention.

"As you all know, we are expecting a news crew this morning. I don't have to tell you how important this is to Angel's Wings. It will boost adoptions and donations alike. But it will also garner us much-needed attention and interest. We are always welcoming progress here, better ways to do this, to do that. We welcome savvy, smart, and nurturing volunteers. We encourage new ideas. And most importantly, we welcome everyone who steps through that door. Because if they are here, then that means they want to make a difference. And we all know what that means, no matter how small the difference is. So," she clapped her hands together, "I want to thank each and every one of you for being here, for making your own differences, and for kindly and selflessly giving Angel's Wings your heart. Let's rock this interview and get ready for one hell of a day."

Her crew burst into applause, and they gathered in the center of the room, chanting, "Who's got heart? We do. Who are we? Angel's Wings. Who's got heart? We do. Who are we? Angel's Wings!" They all clapped in unison and continued the chant as they broke the circle and got back to work. Jayden looked at the clock and ran her hands through her hair. She'd taken the time to blow it dry, and it fell smoothly over one side of her brow. She'd even applied some makeup and a little eyeliner. She noticed that most of her female staff had taken extra time on themselves as well.

"You look devilishly handsome," Mel said, coming up next to her. "I'd eat you alive if you weren't like a sister."

"Gross," Jayden said. "Don't even go there."

"What about me? Don't I look edible?" She held out her hands and turned. Her hair was shimmering and her face was glowing. Her lipstick was perfect, and when she flashed her eyelashes, her hazel eyes sparkled like a pebbled creek bed in the sunlight. It was no wonder women couldn't get enough of her.

"You look drop-dead, as usual."

"Think that reporter will notice? I hear she's into men and women."

Jayden rolled her eyes. She refused to answer.

"They're here!" a volunteer said, running in the entrance like an excited kid. Jayden unclipped her walkie-talkie and spoke.

"News crew has arrived."

"Copy," Faith said.

Jayden and Mel walked to the door. Allie hurried to them,

having handed off the dogs behind the scenes where they would wait to show off their stuff to the entire county. Jayden wrapped an arm around Mel's and Allie's waists. They were the three. The three strong. The ones who ran Angel's Wings, sacrificed, protected, and loved it. Allie grinned and pressed down her polo and shorts. "Do I look okay?"

Jayden nodded and smiled. Allie suddenly seemed very much awake. News attention always got her blood flowing. It got all their blood flowing.

A small group of people approached the door, and Jayden couldn't help but notice her own heart beating a little faster. Allie and Mel pushed open the doors, all smiles, and Jayden focused on black heels, black pleated trousers, a gray silk blouse, and finally, a face that broke into a broad, well-practiced grin.

A hand followed, taking in Jayden's. "Hi, I'm Maureen McCall, Channel Three Action News. You must be Ms. Beaumont?"

Jayden returned the smile and shook her warm hand. "Please call me Jayden."

Maureen's crew followed her in. She released Jayden's hand and began finger-combing her shoulder-length blond hair. "Thank you so much for having us, Jayden. Do you mind if my guys begin setting up?"

Jayden led the way in. "No, not at all."

Maureen nodded, and the guys filtered in behind the counter and began inspecting the office and talking amongst themselves. Jayden caught sight of Mel and Allie and introduced them to Maureen. Mel stammered her words, and Allie couldn't stop grinning.

"I understand you're a no-kill shelter?" Maureen said as she followed Jayden farther in.

"That's correct."

Maureen pressed her deep red lips together as her eyes took everything in. She especially liked the photos, stopping to look at them. "We've heard many good things about this place. And I adopted a dog here last month."

Allie stepped forward. "Yes, of course. You worked with one of our volunteers, Adam. And you adopted Saint, a young pit bull. I was the one who processed you."

Maureen wagged a finger at her. "Allie, right?"

"Yes."

"I remember." She turned back to the photos. "I can't tell you how having Saint has changed my life. Even in a month's time. And…I was very impressed with this place. I understand you're the one responsible," she said, eyeing Jayden with her inquisitive brown eyes.

"We're all responsible," Jayden said.

"Humble. I like it."

"Maureen?" A man with a light sensor interrupted. "We're thinking about shooting over here."

"Yes, of course." She crossed the room as the crew arranged chairs and standing silk trees. Another woman, shorter and extremely focused, approached them all. "We're having some dogs showcased, right?"

"Yes, several," Mel said. "If possible."

"Perfect." She left them again and spoke to the crew, who began fiddling with a camera and lights.

"Producer?" Jayden asked.

"Yes." Maureen turned and studied her. "My right hand."

"These two are mine."

"So I gather." Her eyes scanned them all but then refocused on Jayden. "I'd like to have you as my centerpiece and then have Mel and Allie handle the dogs. I think it would also be great to pan back and get a shot of your staff as we fade out."

Jayden shrugged. "Sure."

Maureen spoke to her group. "Jayden is going to be our main focus, with her friends handling the dogs. I think we should have the rest of the staff stand behind us. What do you think, Kathy? Sound good?"

"You've got the eye," she said, arranging chairs. "Couldn't have said it better myself."

Maureen turned to Jayden. "Great. You ready? I'm just going to ask you basic questions about Angel's Wings and introduce the dogs. May I?" She reached up and brushed an errant strand of Jayden's hair from her brow. "You've got a great look. The camera will love you."

Jayden felt herself heat, and she shifted her gaze from Maureen's heavy one to her staff who were bringing in the dogs. She smiled despite being stared at.

"Here are the real movie stars," she said.

Maureen clasped her hands together as a man clipped on her mic. Then Kathy came over and checked her hair and makeup. She looked to Jayden, but Maureen spoke.

"That one is perfect. Nothing needed."

Kathy blinked. "You're right." She cupped Jayden's elbow and led her to the center chair. Maureen made herself comfortable next to her.

"Just relax and speak to me."

Jayden nodded.

On either side, Mel and Allie stood holding the leashes of three dogs. More waited in the wings. A few barked with excitement.

The crew scrambled and exited the area.

Kathy, who now had on headphones, spoke. "And we're on in ten."

Jayden shifted.

"Live television is a real rush," Maureen said with a wink.

"And we're—" Kathy pointed to Maureen, who spoke into the camera as naturally as if it were her best friend.

"Thanks, Ken. We're coming to you live from Angel's Wings, a no-kill dog shelter north of the valley. And I gotta tell ya, I couldn't be more impressed. Especially with owner and founder, Jayden Beaumont. Jayden, tell us a little bit about your shelter."

Jayden took a deep breath, smiled, and turned on the enthusiasm. She couldn't be prouder of her kennel, her staff, and her animals. And she would do anything for them, including charming the pants off Maureen McCall.

CHAPTER THIRTEEN

Kassandra rounded her desk and hurriedly switched on the library television. The small screen lit with life, and Jayden Beaumont came into view. Kassandra eased back into her chair and nearly missed as Jayden's voice filled the room and her face filled the screen. She looked different—nice, more sophisticated. She had on pressed khaki pants, thick-heeled boots, and a button-down green oxford with the Angel's Wings logo on the breast. Her eyes were intense yet friendly, and she focused on her dogs as she introduced each one.

"Damn, I wish I was there," Kassandra said, shifting in her seat. But she had an early staff meeting that was due to start in ten minutes. Some teachers were already filing into the library, chatting and laughing.

Kassandra turned up the volume, not wanting to miss a word. "We're open seven days a week," Jayden said. "Nine to six on weekdays and eight to seven on Saturday and Sunday." Kassandra stared helplessly at her as the camera panned out to show the reporter and the rest of the staff. "And if you can't adopt right now for whatever reason, we always appreciate donations."

The reporter smiled and reached out to rest a hand on Jayden's knee. "You heard it, folks, directly from the owner

herself. Angel's Wings needs you, and so do these guys."
She motioned to the dogs, who were now sitting and panting.
"Rescuing a dog can change your life. I know it did for me.
Reporting live from north Phoenix, I'm Maureen McCall.
Back to you, Ken."

Kassandra stood, eyes trained on the attractive reporter and
her hand. "What is she doing?" It was probably a job-nicely-
done move, but Kassandra saw it as a bit possessive. If a male
reporter had done something like that, there'd be an uproar. So
why had this woman, this Maureen McCall, done it?

The screen changed back to the news studio. Kassandra
switched it off and held her heating face. Her pulse accelerated,
and something in her gut clenched. She recognized it as the
burn of jealousy. What was happening? A voice from behind
startled her.

"Kassandra, can you clean up the coffee and donuts after
the meeting?"

It was the principal's secretary, Valerie. Not her favorite
person. If the word "snob" was in the dictionary, there'd be a
picture of her right there in the center. Kassandra knew that
cleanup after the meeting was the secretary's responsibility.
After all, Kassandra had to hurry after the meeting to set up for
kindergarten. She had about thirty books to set up for display
on the tables, not to mention readying their checkout cards.
But she found herself nodding, not wanting to rock the boat.

Valerie gave her a smirk and walked away. Kassandra
rolled her eyes. She'd do the cleanup, but it would have to wait
until after kindergarten. The longer she spent at the school, the
more she found herself growing unhappy. She thought again
about moving on, but when she thought of changing schools
and starting over again, she felt defeated and overwhelmed.
And if she were really being honest, she was growing tired of
the library.

She collapsed in her chair and rested her head in her hands. She thought again of Jayden and the news reporter. Did they know each other? What did the hand on the knee mean? Anything? And most importantly, why in the world was it bothering her so much?

She turned on her computer and checked the news and weather, waiting for the meeting to start. It was useless to delve into work until she knew she could. But soon, as the principal began talking about testing and performance, she began to do little things, like organizing and readying the kindergarten checkout cards. The little ones were too young to spell their names or remember their number code. She worked quietly, not wanting to be rude while the principal spoke, but the meeting really didn't pertain to her and she was irritable about Jayden. She couldn't shake it from her mind, and she decided that even though today wasn't her day to volunteer, she'd show up anyway and try to get the scoop on the interview. That idea seemed to calm her a bit, but the anxiety of what she might learn began to eat away at her.

She rubbed tired eyes, not having slept well once again. Lula was doing well and the condo was secure with new top-of-the-line locks, but she still didn't feel safe and she felt ridiculous in sharing her feelings about it. Her friends wanted her to get the security system, but considering doing so did little to ease her thoughts about some strange man having her intimate garments. The meaning behind that could not be good, and it gave her chills along her arms and spine when she thought about it. In fact, she'd started taking her garbage out in the daylight, checking her mail before the sun set. She even installed motion lights on the patios. And some nights, when they came on, she couldn't bear to look and she couldn't bring herself to sleep. But no one knew and she wasn't sure how they'd react if they did.

Secretly, she wished Jayden would bring it up again and maybe even offer to talk to her on the phone every night. But in reality, she'd probably just offer Dax again, and Kassandra wasn't sure what to say. She didn't want to owe anyone for anything, and she knew, just knew, she'd fall in love with Dax and want to keep him. Lula, no doubt, would not approve.

"Kassandra?" Kassandra turned to find one of the teachers whispering over the tall counter. "Can you go heat up my coffee? It's cold and I can't leave the meeting." Kassandra stared at her in disbelief. She rewound the request in her head. Really?

But she tightened her jaw, took the cup, and headed for the lounge. So far the day was just going fabulously. Did she have *step on me* written on her forehead? She tried to be kind, do her work, and lay low. But apparently, others were seeing that differently, and they were trying to take advantage. She thought briefly about dumping the cup and sitting in the lounge until the meeting was over. But Valerie watched her like a hawk, though she had no idea why. She heated the coffee only a little and brought it back. The teacher, whose name she never cared to learn, was off laughing and talking. It seemed the meeting had changed tone. What was she supposed to do with the coffee? Serve her? Kassandra placed it on the counter and hoped like hell it would be frigid by the time she came for it.

She was now in no mood to be so nice. She sat and signed in to the library system and checked her email. More work requests from her boss. More things to organize, oversee, and put into practice. Usually she didn't mind the busywork, but the day had turned dark and she knew she needed to get her mind off work, off people, and off her break-in. The world, it seemed, was just stomping all over her. And it wasn't even first period yet.

How was she going to make it through this day?

The teacher sipped her coffee and made a face. She opened her mouth to speak to Kassandra but then seemed to change her mind. Kassandra smiled at her, daring her.

"Would you mind dumping this out for me?" the teacher said.

Kassandra grabbed a stack of books for the kindergarteners. She walked past her quickly.

"You know where the sink is."

She didn't stop and wait for her response. Instead she busied herself setting up as teachers socialized around her. As she worked she caught sight of two aisles with books strewn on the floor. She wanted to stop and scream. The various meetings held after school brought different groups to meet in the library. And it seemed no one cared if their child ransacked the place. Kassandra sighed. She didn't have time to reshelve before the little ones arrived. Teachers lingered, she saw the kindergarten students at the door as the bell rang. She welcomed them in and problem-solved by choosing three students to help her stand the books up. The rest of the class sat quietly, hoping they'd get chosen for something as well.

"Thank you, guys," she said as she rounded the tables and sat in her reading chair. The kids she'd chosen finished standing their books up and sat. And then, as Kassandra began reading from *Pete the Cat*, the books fell in a line around the table like dominos. Closing her eyes as the kids laughed and pointed, she prayed for the day to end as painlessly as possible. But she knew it was wishful thinking.

CHAPTER FOURTEEN

The lobby in Angel's Wings was packed. People sat, stood, and paced, anxious for a chance to get a look at the available dogs. Jayden hurriedly instructed a volunteer to open the side gate to lead them through to the kennels. She lowered her handheld radio and turned to find more people at the processing desks, their chosen dogs on leashes or sitting in their laps. Small children hopped happily up and down or ran around in small circles. The phones rang off the hook, many having to go to voice mail.

Jayden had almost every staff member on hand, and things were still overwhelming. So far they'd adopted out twenty dogs, and the numbers were only that low because a handful of her staff had to go out and do home checks first. She had been on five. And so far, they'd only had to turn down one person because her apartment was too small for a big dog. Jayden found her a Chihuahua named Juan Pablo instead, so in the end it was a success.

She'd expected the day to be crazy. Even the next couple of weeks. But the sudden rush of business never failed to surprise her or leave her nearly breathless as she somehow pushed through it. She turned back to the lobby as people filed out, following the volunteer to the kennels. Amongst the mass of people, a blond head peeked and bobbed, struggling to come inside. Jayden smiled as Kassandra finally made it through, sunglasses crooked, a small stain on her blouse, and a tousled look to her normally impeccable hair. She sighed with obvious frustration as she tugged off her glasses.

"Rough day?" Jayden asked, leaning on the counter.

Kassandra looked up in surprise. "Huh? Yes. You have no idea."

"Oh, I couldn't imagine," Jayden said with a smile.

Kassandra returned it. "Yeah, I guess not. You don't seem to be busy at all."

"Us? Nah. It's been slow."

She opened the swinging door for her and Kassandra crossed through.

"I wasn't expecting you today," Jayden said.

Kassandra placed her glasses in her purse. "I, uh, saw your interview this morning and I figured you could use the help."

Jayden stared at her flushed cheeks, her smeared eye makeup. Had she been crying? Or maybe sweating? Either way, she looked like she'd seen way better days. "I appreciate that," she said. "And I have just the thing for you." She led the way through the office and into the warehouse. "I had two swamp coolers installed," she said. "So it's much cooler in here now." She smiled. "That way we can work with the dogs in here when it's hot."

"Good idea," Kassandra said.

Jayden motioned for her to follow. They entered the medical room and Jayden crossed to a large kennel in the corner covered by a sheet. "We got these guys today. The family couldn't keep them due to their HOA." She gently removed the sheet to expose a small gray pit bull nursing five puppies. They squirmed for better position and made little whining noises. Kassandra knelt, hand over her mouth.

"They are adorable."

"Mom's a little nervous, as you can imagine. She's also very protective. We haven't been able to get her to eat or drink, so I was hoping you could give it a try. She needs to stay strong for her pups."

"Of course." She smiled. "Oh God, I can smell the puppy smell. I so need the puppy smell after the day I've had."

Jayden knelt next to her. "You okay?"

Kassandra wouldn't meet her gaze. "I'm fine."

"Just one of those days?"

"Unfortunately."

They stood. Kassandra finally looked at her, but only for the briefest of moments. "Your interview looked like it went well."

Jayden nodded. "It did. We've been swamped since opening."

"That reporter," Kassandra said. "She nice?"

"Maureen? Yes, she was very nice. She actually adopted from us not too long ago."

"Oh?"

Jayden cocked her head. "Why are you asking?"

Kassandra walked to the deep sink to wash her hands. "No reason."

Jayden folded her arms over her chest in thought. She wasn't about to tell her that Maureen had called her later in the morning to ask her to dinner. Or that Jayden had flatly turned her down after she'd placed her hand on her leg during the interview. It had been more than a friendly gesture, and as soon as the word "Cut" was said, her hand had lightly traveled upward to her thigh, accompanied by a wink.

Jayden didn't tell her these things because she'd sworn to keep her love life separate from her business relationship with Kassandra. She didn't want anything at all upsetting her, but it seemed this situation had somehow already done so.

"Something wrong?" Jayden asked.

Kassandra dried her hands. "No, nothing's wrong. I just wondered if you two knew each other prior to today."

"No, we didn't."

"Oh."

"Oh?"

"She just seemed a little friendly toward you."

Jayden blinked in confusion. "Why would that matter?"

"It doesn't," Kassandra said quickly. "I just, you know, wondered."

Jayden shook her head as Kassandra snapped on latex gloves and retrieved the wet and dry food from the cabinet. She then grabbed a clean bowl and a large spoon and began mixing the two together.

"Kassandra, I'm confused. I thought we agreed not to talk about things like this. I thought it made you uncomfortable."

She stirred in silence. "We agreed you wouldn't hit on me."

"Oh, right. But my love life, as long as it doesn't concern you, is free game?"

"Love life?" Kassandra looked up, face frozen with shock. "So you do like her?"

Jayden felt like she was falling with nothing to grab on to. The conversation was a black hole, sucking her in and spinning her about. Who knew what realm it would spit her out into.

"You want to know if I like her? Why?"

Kassandra shrugged and refocused on the food, putting it away. "I thought we were friends. And that woman, Maureen, seemed to really like you."

Jayden fell silent. She had no idea what was happening or what it meant. If anything,

"And that comment stung," Kassandra said. "Just so you know."

Jayden sighed. "I'm just confused, Kassandra." She lowered her arms. "But you're right. We are friends. And if you want to talk about our personal lives, I guess it's okay as long as you're okay with it, too."

Kassandra looked at her, the shock gone. But now something else was in its place. Fear.

"Oh, I don't know. Now that you put it that way…"

"Quid pro quo, Kassandra."

"I know, I know." She exhaled heavily. "Fine. Deal."

Jayden grinned. "What do you want to know? If I like her? The answer is no."

"But she likes you?"

"Yes." Kassandra seemed crestfallen, and her reaction sparked a flame inside Jayden. "Does that bother you?"

"What? No. I just suspected."

"I'm not interested," Jayden said. "If that means anything to you." She felt the corner of her mouth lift as she watched Kassandra squirm in place like one of the puppies. "What about you? Anyone interesting in your life?"

"Me? No. I mean I get asked out, but no, no one I'm interested in."

They stood in silence and the puppies grew louder as their mother stood, nose sniffing the air.

"Looks like she's ready to eat," Jayden said. "I'll leave you to it." She smiled again and crossed to the door. She gave Kassandra one last curious look and pushed out the door. The day was turning out to be very interesting indeed.

CHAPTER FIFTEEN

K assandra reentered the medical room with the mother pit bull tugging on her leash.

"Easy, girl. They're right there." She led her to the kennel and opened it, allowing the dog entry. Kassandra closed the door and made sure she settled down comfortably, all five puppies accounted for. They squeaked and squirmed, battling for a nipple. The mother licked each one as if counting them.

Kassandra had spent most of her time with them, caring mostly for the mother. And when she hadn't been doing that, she'd been tailing Gus and Billy as they rushed around the property, doing what needed to be done for a successful close to the day. Kassandra was still in awe at just how many people came out wanting to adopt. Two families even fought over the small poodle she'd been working with. But Jayden had stepped in calmly and worked it out. She gave the dog, Cookie, to the family with older kids because she was so timid. It had been the right move, and Kassandra had warmed at how gracefully she'd handled it. Letting them all know it wasn't about them, it was about Cookie and what was best for her. And then Jayden had introduced the remaining family to a boxer named Bullet. They hadn't originally wanted a big dog, but they had the room and the kids were young and spunky. Perfect for Bullet's energy level. He'd even saturated the kids with kisses upon introduction. With that family happy, Jayden had gone off personally to do the home check. And Kassandra had walked the mother pit bull one last time as the sun set.

"I'm out, Ms. H.," Gus said, as they entered the office. He gave her a half hug and turned his ball cap backward to wipe sweat from his brow.

Kassandra waved and whispered good night in return. He said good-bye to the remaining staff members and disappeared behind the counter. The office was quiet, save for one last family sitting at Allie's desk, filling out information. Kassandra found Jayden at her own desk, head in hands, an exhausted look on her face.

"How's Mama and the pups?" she asked, rubbing her cheeks. She had a fresh tan line around her eyes from her sunglasses.

Kassandra sat, her feet hurting from the few hours she'd worked. She couldn't imagine how Jayden and the other full-time staff felt. "She's fine. Really warming up."

"Good."

Jayden removed her radio and placed it in the charger on her desk. She opened the bottle of water next to it and nearly downed the whole thing. Kassandra looked away as drops fell down into the collar of her polo. She knew she should leave, that there was nothing left for her to do, but she remained sitting as if waiting for something.

Barking came from Jayden's hip and she halfheartedly plucked out her cell phone and answered.

"Brad, man, tell me it's good news."

But her face fell and then tightened with concern. "Where?" Suddenly, she came alive as if a bolt of lightning had struck her with much-needed nutrients and energy. She stood and fumbled for her keys. "I'll be right there." She shoved her phone in her pocket and retrieved more water from the small fridge. She looked at Kassandra. "You up for a rescue?"

"A rescue?" Kassandra watched as she gathered a medical bag and a black duffel that she stuffed the water bottles in.

"There's a dog injured along Northern in west Phoenix. My friend Brad got the call, but he can't get him and he doesn't want to chase him farther out into the desert."

Kassandra stood, suddenly revived herself. "Okay, sure. If you think I can help."

Jayden headed out with Kassandra hot on her heels. They nearly ran across the parking area to a deep red Toyota truck jacked up on rugged-looking tires. Jayden unlocked the doors, tossed the bags in the extended cab, and climbed in. Kassandra did the same and settled into the passenger seat. She noted the GPS, the flat screen, and the radio perched in a charger. Jayden started the engine and peeled out.

"I thought you drove the dually with the air-cooled kennels in the back?" Kassandra asked.

"I usually do. But on desert runs, I have to take this. It maneuvers better." She reached up and pressed a button and Kassandra heard a line ringing. A man answered.

"Where are you?" he asked.

"Just left the rescue. How's our guy?"

"I've stopped the chase. For now, he's staying within sight."

"How bad's the traffic?"

"Off and on. We're at two lanes and it should slow now that rush hour is over."

"Can you tell how bad he's hurt?"

"It's his right hind leg. Looks swollen."

"Any blood?"

"Not that I can see."

"Okay, hang tight." She ended the call and cursed. "The lack of blood concerns me." She glanced at Kassandra.

"Why?"

"Could be a snake bite."

"Oh, shit." Kassandra hadn't even considered that. "Do you see a lot of those?"

"I've seen a handful. If he's not treated real soon, he'll die."

Kassandra swallowed hard and stared at the road. Could she handle seeing a dog die? A dog suffering? Could she handle this? She'd already agreed to come along to help, so help was what she had to do. But her stomach was flip-flopping and a sense of panicked dread was overcoming her. So much so that she stared in silence until they arrived and only then did she jerk to attention as Jayden touched her arm.

"We're here."

Kassandra nodded. Jayden turned on her hazard lights and drove up next to the animal control vehicle that was parked off in the dirt shoulder on the left side of the road. Two men sat inside. Night had settled and there were no streetlights. Empty desert stretched for what seemed like miles.

Jayden eased down her window and gave a nod.

"He's right out there at our ten o'clock," the driver said.

Jayden leaned out the window, searching. "Got him."

Kassandra tried, but she couldn't see him.

"You guys go ahead and pull up a little. I'm going to go around behind him." Jayden put the truck in reverse and backed away and then drove into the desert slowly. Kassandra scanned the dirt in the cones of light, desperate to find the dog.

"There," Jayden said, pointing to the right. She turned then and parked at an angle, turning on her overhead KC lights. The dog started, tried to move, but failed. He was panting furiously and nearly skin and bones. He looked to be a husky mix of some sort.

Kassandra reached for the doorknob with a shaky hand.

"No, don't." Jayden grabbed her shoulder. "Not yet." She reached behind her and grabbed a long pole with a noose on the end. Then she retrieved black gloves, wrist guards, and a mesh muzzle. She slung the medical bag across her chest like a satchel. "Okay, I'm going first, slowly. Right now, I don't think he can move. But just in case, I don't want to overwhelm him or cause him to run."

"Okay."

Jayden plucked the radio and gave the same instructions to Brad, also mentioning the possible snakebite to which Brad said he was already prepared for. Then Jayden carefully exited the vehicle and approached the wary dog. Again, he tried to rise, but again he fell, unable to stand. He barked at Jayden nervously as she grew closer, walking slowly with her palms out. She held the pole with the noose upright, and as she neared him she began talking softly to him. At about ten feet away, Jayden stopped and held her hands out into a stop position to both vehicles. Kassandra remained still, watching intently.

Jayden stepped closer, lowered the pole, and quickly noosed the dog, who began whining and squirming. Jayden crawled to him, over him, and held on to his snout from behind. She eased the mesh muzzle onto him and then stroked him long and slow, calming him. She leaned and looked at his leg. She waved Brad out.

"Looks like a bite," she said as Brad jumped from his truck with a medical box. He, too, approached carefully, not wanting to scare the dog. Kassandra watched anxiously as Brad examined his lower leg and checked his vitals. He then motioned for his partner, who joined the group, carrying a stretcher.

Jayden continued to hold the dog in her arms, speaking softly, stroking his neck. Kassandra couldn't tear her eyes away from the gentle scene playing out before her. And soon they had the dog on the stretcher, heading for the animal control truck. Jayden motioned for her to join.

Kassandra crawled from the truck hesitantly. She trotted through the desert to the other vehicle. The three were working on the dog, inserting an IV. Kassandra looked away from his trembling body. She covered her mouth and closed her eyes.

The trio spoke quickly, worked efficiently, and she could hear them loading the dog up for transport. Jayden was on the phone with an emergency clinic wanting to bring the dog there. She was afraid animal control would put him down, and she wanted him to have the best care.

Kassandra drowned out the rest until a gentle hand touched her shoulder. Jayden came to a stand before her. "They are taking him to a friend of mine. She runs a twenty-four-hour emergency clinic."

"Will he make it?" Kassandra's heart just tore for him, and all she could do was imagine a similar scenario as Jayden and Brad had saved Lula.

"I think so."

"How do you know?"

"I don't for sure. But I've seen a lot. And this one is a fighter."

Kassandra felt a warm hand slide into hers. She inhaled sharply as she met Jayden's piercing eyes.

"You're not okay, are you?"

Kassandra struggled for words. "I'm fine. I'm just worried about him, and seeing him and listening to you guys work on him—"

"It made you think of Lula."

"Yes."

Jayden led them back to her truck as Brad and his partner quickly drove away. Kassandra felt safe, warm as they held hands and walked. Jayden was so fierce and so strong, yet she was so incredibly gentle. It was a dichotomy she couldn't quite grasp. How could a person be so many things? Have so many layers? Be so special to both humans and animals alike?

"I think of all the dogs I love when I try to save one. And then, as I get down to business, I think of only one thing. Saving them. The rest, the emotion, the heartache, it goes and I can do my job."

"What if they don't make it?"

They stood at the passenger door and Jayden faced her, holding both hands. "Then I send them off as peacefully as I can."

Kassandra fought tears.

Jayden squeezed her hands. "It's not a job for everyone." She opened the door for her. "I'll drive you back to your car."

Kassandra stepped up inside the truck. "No. I want to go with you. I want to be there for this dog."

"You sure?" Jayden rested a hand on her knee as she studied her.

Kassandra nodded. "Yes. I've never been more sure of anything."

Chapter Sixteen

Jayden drove in silence as Kassandra slept propped up against the passenger door. Her breathing was soft and she was snoring lightly with cute little puffs of air. The evening had been dramatic, and Kassandra had handled it well, considering it was her first time saving a dog near death. Jayden had seen tears slip down her face only once, and that was when they were leaving the dog for the night. Kassandra seemed to be a sensitive soul, mostly quiet and unassuming, but very observant and intelligent. She learned quickly, and once at the clinic didn't hesitate to jump in and help, holding the dog and soothing him as they gave him the antivenom. She'd held him for the next hour, praying he would make it. Jayden had been impressed. She'd seen a lot in her line of work, and many grown women couldn't handle a situation like that. Many grown men couldn't either. It took strength, courage, and an understanding of life and loss. Kassandra seemed to understand that he was pain free now, and if he did pass, he would do so peacefully. Thankfully, though, the dog was recovering and resting. But Jayden knew he still had a long road ahead of him, considering his physical condition before the bite.

She hoped like hell he'd make it, hoped Kassandra would get to see the difference they made. But for now, they were both exhausted and Jayden had offered to take Kassandra directly home. Lula needed her, and Jayden didn't trust Kassandra to drive in her exhausted state. She'd had a hard day and even mumbled a little about it as they had waited at the emergency clinic. Some coworkers were giving her a hard time and she wasn't sleeping well.

Jayden wanted to insist on her taking Dax, but she held back. Kassandra had to make up her own mind.

Jayden gently shook her awake as she pulled into her complex. Kassandra straightened, but her eyes kept falling closed. Jayden wondered just how many nights she'd gone without sleep. She killed the engine and rounded the truck to help her out.

"Are you walking me to my door?"

"Yes." Jayden held out a protective arm, afraid she might stumble.

"There's no need. I can take care of myself, you know."

"I know. I'm just being polite. Making sure you're in safe and sound."

They walked down a quiet sidewalk to a patio with a thigh-high gate. Jayden unlatched it as Kassandra dug in her pocket for her keys. A motion light came on, and Kassandra focused on the lock. Something, however, caught Jayden's eye.

"Someone's got a secret admirer." Jayden held up the bouquet of flowers from the patio chair. Kassandra blinked at them in apparent disbelief. Her face reddened and then went chalk white.

Jayden stepped to her. "Something wrong?"

"Is there a card? Anything?"

Jayden checked the chair, the ground. "No."

"Oh, God." Kassandra pushed open her door and hurried inside. Jayden followed, confused.

"What is it? What's wrong?" The spark of jealousy that

kept trying to ignite in her gut was shoved from her mind by Kassandra's reaction.

Kassandra lifted an excited Lula and paced her living room. Jayden closed the door and watched helplessly as fear overcame her.

"I don't know who they're from," she said.

Jayden noticed that all the lights were on in the house. All the blinds closed. There were two deadbolt locks on the door along with what looked like door opening sensors. The home was decorated nicely and well kept, but Jayden could sense the uncertainty of its safety. For Kassandra's sake, she tried not to assume the worst.

"Maybe a neighbor you're friends with?"

Kassandra shook her head. "They always leave a note if they leave me something."

"Maybe they forgot this time."

"You don't understand." She set Lula on the couch and rubbed her forehead.

"What am I not getting?"

Kassandra stopped and looked at her. "If they were from anyone I knew, there'd be a note or a message on my door or my phone. I'm not dating. I have no man asking me out…"

Jayden sank down onto the couch.

"Jayden, whoever broke into my house…he took things. Personal things. Intimate things."

Jayden stared at her as heat rose up to her face. "You're sure?"

"Positive."

"Did you tell the police?"

Kassandra sighed and sank down on the opposite side. Lula hopped from one end to the other, giving them both kisses. "By the time I realized it, I was too embarrassed to call."

"Kassandra, you need to tell them. They need to know this."

"Why? So they can keep a lookout for my panties?"

Jayden stood, walked to the windows, and checked to make sure they were secure and locked. Now she was beginning to feel more than uncertain.

"No, so they can ask around to see if other women are being targeted. Or if anyone has seen a Peeping Tom."

"A Peeping Tom? You mean he might have been... watching me?"

Jayden crossed to the two bedrooms and checked the windows there. "I don't know. But it wouldn't hurt if the cops checked it out. Has anyone been lurking? Have you noticed anything unusual?"

Kassandra was silent for a moment. "I sometimes notice that my motion lights come on at night."

Jayden thought quickly. Tonight, they'd been well into the patio before they came on. But she didn't say anything more. It wouldn't do any good for both of them to panic. She returned to the living room, saw the mortified look on Kassandra's face, and her heart melted. She was so frightened and tired. Her normally sparkling eyes were dark and deep. "How long has it been since you've had sleep?"

"I don't know." She ran a limp hand through her short hair. "A couple of days."

Jayden eased down next to her. "I want to stay the night."

Kassandra looked at her quickly. "You what?"

"I'll sleep out here, keep an eye on things, and you can sleep."

Kassandra touched her neck as if she'd felt something there, a caress perhaps. Her eyes were wide. "I'm fine, really. I have the new locks..."

"Yet you still aren't sleeping. And now the flowers." She reached out and touched her hand. "Let me do this for you."

Kassandra inhaled sharply at the contact. Jayden noticed, but she didn't dare move. The moment was heavy, pivotal. Jayden suspected Kassandra's attraction, but she didn't want to risk being wrong. She wanted Kassandra to trust her. She wanted her in her life any way she could have her. Even if that meant being close friends.

"We're both filthy," Kassandra finally said, surprising her. "We need to shower."

Jayden pulled her hand away, embarrassed by the thought of them showering together. She cleared her throat, trying to get the image out of her mind.

"I'm okay as is. I can sleep on the floor."

"No, you won't. If you're going to stay, you're going to be comfortable."

"So I'm staying, then?"

Kassandra nodded. "If you'd like. Will your dogs be okay?"

"My guys? Yeah, they'll be fine. Allie's there. She knew I'd be out all night with the rescue. Sometimes I hang at the vet clinic until the dog's able to be released."

"That's dedication," Kassandra said softly. "Don't you ever take a break? Take time for you?"

"I don't need to," she said. "At least I don't think so."

"Maybe you should try."

Jayden looked at her, curious. "Do you think I'm too far in?"

"I haven't known you for very long. But from what I've seen…it seems you do everything. You're always busy or out on a call. Do you sleep?"

Jayden laughed. "I do."

"Guess I'll have to witness that to believe it."

She stood and disappeared into the second bedroom. Jayden assumed it was her study, with a nice desk and two large bookshelves. Movie posters were framed and hung on the walls, most of them classic thrillers and noirs. Jayden wanted to sit in there, choose a book, and read for hours. She imagined Kassandra doing just that, and her heart warmed.

Kassandra returned, caught her smiling blissfully, and cocked her head. For whatever reason, she chose not to ask her about it.

"You can shower in there," she said, referring to the bathroom in the study. "I laid out some necessities for you." She handed over a small pile of clothes and towels. "I know it's not great and probably not what you normally sleep in, but all I have are cotton nightgowns."

Jayden laughed but stopped when she realized she was serious. "I definitely do not wear those. You're right about that."

"My pajamas are too small; you'd be uncomfortable. What do you normally sleep in?"

Jayden took the small pile from her. "My birthday suit."

"Oh." Kassandra looked away.

"Don't worry, I won't do that here."

Kassandra rubbed the back of her neck. "I'll, um, just make your bed on the couch while you shower."

Jayden smiled as she watched her move nervously around the living room. "Thanks, Kassandra. For letting me stay and help."

Kassandra looked up. "Thank you, for caring."

Jayden held her gaze for a moment and then entered the bathroom to shower. She'd imagined this scenario more than once, and now that it was here, she wasn't quite prepared for just how strongly she felt for her. Not just a physical attraction, but a protectiveness, a longing to just hold her and listen to her breathe in peace.

She turned on the faucet and slipped out of her shoes. She might not be able to hold her, or express how deeply she felt, but she could protect her and give her some peace of mind. And that, she realized, was the most important thing.

Chapter Seventeen

Kassandra awoke to morning Lula kisses. She rolled to her side and squinted at the red numbers on her clock. Her alarm would go off in an hour. Her eyes felt heavy, and she was just about to fall back asleep when she smelled something. She sat up. Pancakes. She was sure of it.

"Jayden," she whispered, suddenly remembering she had stayed over.

Lula jumped from the bed and scratched at the closed door. Kassandra followed her, opening the door and walking to the kitchen. Jayden was standing at the stove staring at a bubbling circle of batter and wearing one of Kassandra's nightgowns. Lula rushed to kiss her ankles.

"Do not…" Jayden said without turning, "laugh at me."

Kassandra pressed her lips together. "Okay."

"This nightgown is way too short for me, and it feels way too close to a dress." She tugged on it as if that would somehow make it remain lower on her mid-thigh.

"You look nice." Kassandra couldn't seem to look away from her long, tanned legs. Jayden flipped the batter with a spatula and turned. Kassandra smiled. Jayden was wearing the Garfield gown. The one that showed Garfield wearing a scowl and holding a mug of coffee. It said "I hate mornings." The caption seemed to fit her as she stood with her hand on her hip, scowl on her face, dark hair disheveled.

"I told you not to laugh."

"I'm sorry. It's just…you look so cute."

Jayden rolled her eyes. "Where in the world did you put my clothes?"

"Oh, I washed them. They're in the dryer." She turned to go get them.

"Don't. It can wait until after we eat."

Kassandra joined her at the small table next to the plantation blinds. Normally, Kassandra would open them for breakfast, but she was still uncomfortable in thinking that someone might be watching her.

"You didn't have to go to all this trouble," she said, feeling a little guilty. After all, Jayden was her guest.

"Nonsense. I love this. Besides, you look like you could use a good meal." She sat across from her and sipped her orange juice.

Kassandra did the same, and they both dug into their pancakes and small talk. Kassandra kept looking up at her, secretly thrilled that she was there, sitting across from her, voice still scratchy from sleep. Her hair stood like a Mohawk, and her eyes seemed to penetrate in the kitchen light. She was breathtaking. Kassandra realized she never looked at Scott and felt this way. Was he just not the man for her…or were men in general not for her?

"What are you thinking about?" Jayden asked with a smile. "You look intense."

Kassandra forked a bite of egg. "Nothing, just…" Should she tell her about Scott?

"Just…?"

Kassandra licked her lips, suddenly nervous. "I was thinking about my ex-husband."

Jayden tried to hide her brief surprise, but Kassandra saw it.

"I'm sorry. I just had no idea you had been married."

"I have."

"You don't sound too happy about it."

"I'm not. I mean, I wasn't. I just realize it more and more as time goes on."

Jayden drank more juice. "Did he hurt you?"

"Oh, no. Nothing like that. He just…I just…I don't know. He was so apathetic, and eventually, I too began not to care. We lived that way for a year, just going through the motions. Like robots. No feelings, no connection. Just existing in the same house."

"Sounds like my worst nightmare," Jayden said.

"It wasn't a nightmare, but it was…uncomfortable. And it seemed never ending, like we were trapped that way. He didn't want to rock the boat to escape and neither did I. Because, honestly, we did care about one another. Just not in a passionate way."

Jayden was watching her closely. "You're very kind," she said. "The way you talk about people. Even those that have done you wrong or caused you pain."

"I don't know about that. You haven't seen me drive."

Jayden laughed and gathered their plates.

"No, let me," Kassandra said, rising. She followed her to the sink, but Jayden wouldn't have it.

"Will you go relax? I've got this. Let someone do for you for a change."

The words startled Kassandra, and she stopped. She looked into Jayden's eyes. She knew she should look away, but she couldn't. She was being pulled in. By her presence, her words, and those goddamned gray eyes.

"Kassandra," Jayden whispered.

But Kassandra stopped her, placing a single finger upon her lips. Then she rose to her tiptoes and kissed her. It was delicate at first, and Kassandra closed her eyes, unsure if the moment was real or imagined. When Jayden kissed back oh so gently and moaned, Kassandra knew it was real, and she made her own small noise of approval. Jayden responded by wrapping her arms around her and pulling her close. Kassandra pressed harder, began slowly framing Jayden's lips with her own. They both struggled for breath when it grew from gentle and pressing to heated and aggressive. Kassandra felt Jayden's tongue lightly probe, and it was as if a bolt of electricity had shot up her spine. It took all her willpower not to seek back with her own. But she could feel herself trembling, hear their bated breath, feel the moans coming up from her chest. If she melted and gave in there'd be no stopping. The realization sent a rush of warmth between her legs, but it also terrified the tiny remaining rational part of her. She couldn't make love to Jayden. She wouldn't even know where to begin. She couldn't make love to anyone, for that matter, because it meant letting them in. And they always failed her. Every single time. She couldn't afford a mess like that anymore. And she definitely didn't want a mess with Jayden. She cared way too much about her.

Kassandra felt Jayden's tongue seek again, and her center began to throb. She had to stop, had to stop now or she might very well orgasm right there on the spot. She pulled away and covered her lips, the hot tingling still lingering.

"Oh. Oh, God." She turned, completely overwhelmed at her body's reaction.

Jayden seemed to struggle for the right words. "It's okay," she said.

"I don't know what came over me." What the hell had just happened? Dear God. And why was her body still reacting when they weren't even touching?

"Kassandra, you don't have to apologize. It was... beautiful. You are beautiful."

"I can't do this," she said before Jayden could melt her heart with any more sweet words. "I can't." She hurried from the kitchen to her bedroom where she closed the door. Jayden chased after her.

"Kassandra, what is it? What's wrong?" She knocked lightly. "Can you talk to me?"

"I'm sorry, Jayden. I can't. I can't do this."

"Do what?"

"Feel this way."

"Why?"

"I just can't."

"Because I'm a woman?"

Was it because she was a woman? Partly. But that wasn't the whole story.

"Because...because you are everything." It made sense to her, but she knew it wouldn't to Jayden.

"I'll go," she said. "I don't want you to be upset."

Kassandra heard her fumbling with the dryer. She opened the door to try to explain the madness that was her, but she found her standing in nothing but her panties. They both froze. Kassandra took her in all at once, flushed profusely, forgot to breathe, and then closed the door again.

"Oh, God." She collapsed against the door. "Holy shit." Small taut breasts, the etched muscles of her torso, the strength in her shoulders and arms—it all made her head spin.

She heard Lula scratching at the door, but she didn't open it. If she did she knew she'd throw herself in Jayden's arms and lose all control.

"I'm going now," she heard Jayden say softly.

"Okay." Her heart tore in two and she closed her eyes.

"I'm sorry," she offered.

"You didn't do anything wrong," Kassandra said. "This is me. All me."

"Can I call you later? Check on you?"

"It's probably best if you didn't. Best for you."

"I'm not worried about me."

But Kassandra didn't respond; she couldn't find the right words. There were no right words for her behavior.

"What about your car?"

Kassandra thought quickly. "My friend Wendy will take me to get it."

There was a brief pause. "Kassandra, I will be here. Please don't forget that. I'm not going anywhere."

The words were powerful and meant more to Kassandra than she ever could've imagined. But while they soothed her and reached her down deep, they also brought up bad memories. She felt as though she was bleeding out, all over the carpet. She heard her walk out the door, heard a confused Lula whine and scratch. She stood, opened the door, and hurried to the window. She watched as Jayden hurried to her truck. She lifted Lula and buried her face in her scent.

"I've really done it this time, Luls. I've really fucked up. I've gone and fallen for a woman."

CHAPTER EIGHTEEN

A re you going to tell me what's up your ass or do I have to guess?" Mel slid a bottle of Corona to her. They were sitting at the bar in a sports grill. Jayden took a few big sips and then pushed in her slice of lime. She was on her third beer, some ball team was in the third quarter, and Mel was asking her for the third time.

"Ha. Threes. I like threes. They say things happen in threes."

Mel lowered her beer and stared at her. "What the fuck? Are you sick?" She felt her forehead.

Jayden swatted her away. "I'm fine. I'm just trying to enjoy the game."

"You don't like sports, Jayden. They bore you. Just like sitting here drinking does."

"So."

"So, what the hell is wrong? You've been working yourself to death and then challenging the devil himself with drinking afterward. You're a mess."

Jayden met her gaze, feeling fierce. "I'm fine. Things are perfectly well under control. The rescue, the dogs, the volunteers. I've got it all covered."

Mel wasn't buying it. "You're hiding."

Jayden let out a raucous laugh. "Hiding! From what?"

"Your pain."

Jayden rolled her eyes and drank some more. "I don't have time for pain, you know that. Too much to do."

Mel pushed away both their beers. "Come on, let's get you home."

"No, no, no. I wanna stay. A call might come in."

"Jayden, it's late and you're driving down buzzed bypass and headed for drunk highway. There's no way you're going on a call."

"Then who will?"

"I don't know, me? One of the other volunteers or staff? You know, all these people you have in your corner that you don't utilize enough."

She wrapped a strong arm around her waist and lifted. Jayden stood, embarrassed. "Get off of me. I know how to walk."

"Then do it, hotshot." Mel led the way out of the dim bar and into the dark night. Jayden fished her keys out of her pocket and unlocked her truck. She smiled as she walked, the alcohol making her feel warm and carefree. But Mel ruined her mood when she forcefully took the keys from her and climbed in behind the wheel. She eyed her as Jayden started to protest. "Don't give me any lip, Beaumont. Just get your ass in here."

Jayden held up her hands. "Whoa, whoa. No need to get pissy. I'm coming." She opened the door and pulled herself into the lifted truck. She closed the door and tried a few times to master the seat belt. "You don't have to embarrass me, you know."

"Embarrass you? Right, I wouldn't dream of it." She started the vehicle and backed out, then nearly peeled out of the parking lot.

"What's your problem?"

Mel shook her head. "You. You're my problem." She looked at her and Jayden noted the stone look to her face. She was seriously pissed. Jayden swallowed, knowing what was coming.

"You fell in love with a straight woman, a volunteer. And surprise! She's not into you. She turned you down. She teased you. Gave you a little taste and then freaked out. I could've written a damn book on this, Jayden. How many times did I tell you to leave her alone? Huh? And now she's upset and she's not coming back. You're torn into a million pieces, but you won't admit it. You just work, work, work, and drink, drink, drink. The kids are noticing, Jayden. Do you realize that?"

Jayden looked at her hard. "They don't know everything. They just think they do."

"Yes, my friend, they do. They're smart. They know it's because of Kassandra. They can add one plus one and get two. We all can."

Jayden's heart fell to her churning gut. She didn't want the kids to know. They didn't need to know such things. They had enough to deal with. But here she was continuing to act like a zombie and drink like a fish. Showing up early in the morning with her hair tousled from a drunken stupor and a horrible hangover running through her blood. But they couldn't know that, right? She never drank in front of them. And she'd been telling them she hadn't been feeling well.

"They know you're drinking, Jayden," Mel said softly, as if reading her mind. "Gus sees the beer cans when he does the garbage."

Jayden palmed her forehead and felt nauseous. "Shit." What kind of role model was she being? What the hell was she doing? "Shit!" She pounded the door with her fist.

Mel said nothing; she didn't need to. Jayden was finally hearing her. She could wallow all she wanted to about

Kassandra and drink herself to death. But not when she had kids to look after. She wasn't afforded that kind of bad behavior. She was responsible, not only for the kids but for the dogs. For everything. And even though she'd been working hard, she hadn't really been present. Her mind was constantly on Kassandra. What did her absence mean? Why wouldn't she answer the phone? What had she done wrong?

No wonder the kids were pissed at her. Not only were they blaming her for Kassandra's continued absence, they were watching her self-destruct without a care in the world.

"They fucking hate me right now," she said. "And I don't blame them." She could still hear Gus as he had stalked toward her.

"What did you do? What did you say? Did you hit on her? Scare her away? Yo, she's not like you, Beaumont. She's not someone who takes things like relationships lightly. She cares. She really cares. And you know, she's too good for you. She's deserves better than some player."

His words had crushed her, but she knew he was right. She'd waved him off, told him he didn't know all that he thought he did. Yet somehow he did know. And she just drank his words away.

"I need to talk to them," she said. "I'll talk to them tomorrow."

"Good idea."

"I'm sorry, Mel."

"Don't be sorry. Just stop it."

"I can't help how I feel. I can't help that I care so much about her."

"Can't help that you seriously want to jump her bones?"

Jayden shook her head. "It's more than that, Mel. It's different with her. So different."

Mel drove on, jaw stern. "You know I'm not trying to be

an ass," she said. "I'm just worried about you. I don't doubt your feelings or insist you not have them. I just can't stand to watch you hurt and self-destruct. This is new territory for me. I'm not used to seeing you like this. The last time…was when Rose died."

Jayden gripped the armrest on the door and closed her eyes. The loss of her grandmother had nearly killed her. She'd been her mother, her best friend. Everything a kid could possibly ask for. Her loss left a deep hole, and Jayden still hadn't filled it yet, she'd just found a way to maneuver around it. Mel was right, though. She'd been a wreck. Working herself to the bone until she was often dehydrated, weary, and ready for collapse. It hadn't taken her team long to corner her, force her to rest and hydrate and face her loss. It had been the most difficult time in her life. And while she had faced her loss, she still couldn't believe her grandmother was gone. It was as if she were on a long trip and she'd show up any day, smiling, asking for a hot cup of coffee.

Jayden had held her hand as she'd passed. Had been by her side for weeks as she slowly slipped further and further away. So her death should feel real. Her grief had been real. But why did she not feel her loss now?

"I'm worried, Jay," Mel said. "I don't want to lose you to that abyss again."

"I understand."

"That was a real rough time. For all of us."

"Yes."

"Are you going to be okay? Now, I mean? Or do we have to put you on lockdown?"

Jayden sighed. "I'll be fine."

Mel drove on in silence. "I'm sorry about Kassandra. She was nice."

"Yes, she was."

"You just need to get your mind off her. Get out. Get shaking."

"I'm not sure I'm ready."

"You have to make yourself." She looked over at her. "Go to that eighties party with me."

Jayden grimaced. "No, I'm not up for that."

"Never know until you show."

"Did you just make that up?"

"Maybe."

Jayden laughed, but it fell into aching silence as she once again thought of Kassandra and the way she'd felt in her arms and against her lips. It had felt so right. So perfect. As if they were made for one another. Had Kassandra not felt it? It seemed unlikely, considering her strong reaction. It seemed more like she was afraid. Jayden wished she could somehow help. But Kassandra was making it clear with her silence that she didn't want her help or anything else from her. And that tore into her each time she thought about it.

"What do you say? Will you go?"

Jayden looked out the window as her heart tore once again. "I'll think about it." She'd do anything to make the pain stop.

Chapter Nineteen

I don't think I should go back to Angel's Wings," Kassandra said, sipping her wine. It had been another tough day, and Tony hadn't come to school. He was coming sporadically now, and she'd argued with the counselor again over him and had gotten nowhere. She'd received the call from Child Protective Services over a week ago, and she knew they were planning a surprise home visit. But Tony had said nothing, just did his usual complaining. She had a feeling he wasn't spending much time there.

"Why not?" Katelynn asked. "I thought you loved it."

Kassandra paused. "I do. I mean I did. But I just don't think it's a good idea." Truth was, she hadn't been in a couple of weeks. She just couldn't bring herself to go. She knew she'd take one look at Jayden and crumble.

Her friends looked at one another knowingly and then looked back at her.

"What?" Kassandra had never seen them look like that before.

"Is it because of Jayden?"

Kassandra nearly knocked over her wine. "No. No, of course not." How could they possibly know? She'd only spoken of Jayden in passing. Hadn't she? Come to think of it, she did talk about her a lot. But then again they worked together nearly every day she was at the kennel. It was only natural that she speak of someone she spent a lot of time with. Right? She stared down at the white tablecloth.

"Then what is it?"

Kassandra fingered her wineglass, then turned it, staring at the red.

"So, I'm here, it's happy hour." She smiled, trying to change the subject.

Katelynn didn't look too pleased at her attempt. "Did something happen between the two of you?"

Kassandra once again stared at her wineglass. "No." She took a sip.

"Then what upset you? What did she do?"

"Nothing." She sipped again and forced a smile. "Jayden is a nice person." They couldn't possibly know. No way. They were lesbians, not mind readers.

"You know, Kassandra, if you're having feelings for her, we understand what that feels like."

"Believe it or not, we kinda do. Being lesbians and all."

Kassandra felt her eyes widen. She tried to protest but instead pressed her lips together and twisted the stem on her wineglass. She knew they would understand, but what if she didn't? She had no idea what any of this meant. So how could she voice it? Explain it?

"I just…I think I got too emotionally involved. With the dogs. That's all."

"And you don't want to return to the shelter? If anything, I think that shows you care. And surely Jayden or someone can help you through that."

"Wait a minute. I thought you were learning to handle that better. You know, since the night of that rescue? You said you had really grown a lot, having to face death with that young dog. You said even Jayden was impressed."

Kassandra sighed, growing frustrated.

"I'm just in a strange place right now. I need more time to myself."

"But you were making such a difference. And you were happier. You looked as though you'd been lit up from the inside."

"I just enjoyed seeing the boys."

"And the dogs," Katelynn added.

"And maybe even…Jayden?" Wendy asked.

Kassandra glanced up quickly. Her mouth went dry. She tried, but she could think of nothing to counter it. She knew her wall was crumbling and her friends were watching it fall piece by tiny piece. They wanted in and they were using truth and understanding to penetrate.

"I remember the first woman I had feelings for. God, I didn't know what was happening to me. I thought I was going insane. I couldn't stop thinking about her," Wendy said.

"You can't sleep, you can't eat. You want nothing more than to just be with her."

Kassandra finished off her wine and cleared her nervous throat. They were talking about her and how she felt about Jayden. It was the same. How could they be so dead-on?

"I'm…okay, really."

"You're okay, all right. You've been on cloud nine. You were high on her."

"Until now."

Kassandra closed her eyes. "Can we just please talk about something else? Anything else."

Katelynn touched her hand. "I think you need to talk about this."

Kassandra didn't know what to say. While she trusted her friends, she didn't really trust herself. If she admitted her feelings, it would make things real. It would mean Jayden had gotten in and she'd have to deal with it. Her heart just couldn't take it.

"I like Jayden, yes. But nothing is going on. We're just friends and that's how it's going to remain."

"So you'll go back to the kennel?"

Kassandra smiled at their persistence. Could she go back? She'd told herself Jayden was nothing but a friend. That she could handle it. She was stronger now, in control of her thoughts and feelings.

"Sure."

"Great. I think you'll be happy with this decision," Katelynn said.

"Me too." Wendy smiled.

Kassandra rolled her eyes. "As if I had a choice with you two breathing down my neck."

"That's right. Don't you forget it, either."

"We just want your happiness."

"I know."

"And someday, we hope you'll let us in."

"I do."

"All the way."

Kassandra saw the sincerity on their faces. She was truly grateful for them and she knew they'd never intentionally hurt her. Maybe someday she could trust enough to tell them everything.

"Hey, look who's here."

Three new people appeared and Katelynn and Wendy both stood and gave hugs. Two were women, and they shook hands with Kassandra, pulling out chairs to sit next to her. The man sat next to her friends and he politely shook her hand also. His name was Brian, and Kassandra remembered that this was the man Katelynn and Wendy had wanted her to meet.

"I've heard so much about you," he said with a gentle

smile. Then a perplexed look came over his face. "Haven't we met?"

Kassandra blinked, unsure. He did look a little familiar. "I'm not sure."

He snapped his fingers. "Yes, I think you live in my complex. Garden Grove?"

Kassandra laughed. "Yes, of course. I run into you getting the mail some days."

He opened his straw and drank from the glass of ice water the waiter brought. "I don't think I could forget a face like yours." He smiled again.

Kassandra looked to Katelynn and Wendy, who looked a little uneasy, as if they thought she might bolt at any second.

"We've told Kassandra a lot about you."

"Oh, no." His blue eyes shined and he had a warm smile. But Kassandra wasn't moved by him. His haircut was nice, his shirt pressed, along with his pants. And she knew most women would find him attractive, but she didn't. His arms were hairy, not at all smooth and tanned like Jayden's. He had a five o'clock shadow, and she knew from experience how rough it would feel on her skin.

She'd been dreaming of soft, smooth, warm skin on skin. She knew that kissing this man would be nothing like kissing Jayden.

"Kassie?"

Kassandra refocused, unaware that she'd been daydreaming.

"You okay?"

"Yes, fine." The waiter had brought her more wine. She sipped, silently cursing herself for thinking of Jayden again. But truth was truth. She didn't want this man, or any other man.

Brian, though, seemed to have other ideas. He asked her

question after question, as if they were on a date. She answered, keeping her answers brief. She didn't want to be rude, but she was more interested in the conversation the women were having. The two women were gay, just like her friends, and they were discussing relationships and dating.

Kassandra found herself wanting to know everything.

Brian seemed to want her all to himself, though, and he kept on with the questions. When he finally asked her out, she was frustrated and a little inebriated.

"So what do you think? Maybe we could go for a hike and picnic at this creek I know of."

"That sounds nice," Wendy said. "Which creek, Brian?"

"Fossil Creek."

Kassandra felt herself heat with frustration and anger. Everyone was assuming she wanted or that she should date this guy. What she wanted—what she really wanted—she had chosen to let go and that angered her even more. So she decided to put it all to rest.

"I'm not dating men anymore."

Everyone fell silent. Brian looked shocked, his face crestfallen. All four women searched her face madly, looking for answers, a reason, an explanation. Then Wendy laughed and clapped her hands.

"Well, amen, sister." She wrapped an arm around her and gave her a squeeze. "I believe she has just spoken her truth."

"I guess she has," Katelynn said.

Brian sat staring at his fork, trying to look up and smile from time to time, as if he was taking it all in stride.

"Kassie, would you mind coming with me to the restroom?" Wendy asked.

Kassandra placed her napkin on the table and rose. She followed her to the front of the restaurant where people were mingling in the crowded bar.

"What's going on? What was that all about?"

"I just told the truth. It's what you wanted. For me to share everything."

Wendy nodded, rubbing the back of her neck as if she didn't know what to do.

"Yes, you certainly did. Why didn't you say something sooner?"

"Because I didn't know until just now."

"You want to date women now?"

Kassandra grew frustrated again. "I just don't want to date men. Can't that be good enough for now?"

"Is this about Jayden?" She met her gaze and seemed to see something. "It is, isn't it? I should've known." She held her hands. "You have real feelings for her, don't you? You don't have to answer. Just know that we are here for you. We understand."

Kassandra looked away, too afraid she would tear up. "I want to know things," she confessed.

"I know. Honey, I know. You probably have a million questions."

"But I'm afraid. I'm afraid knowing will only make it worse."

"You mean make your feelings stronger?"

"Yes." Kassandra felt her knees weaken with relief. "And I don't want them to get worse. I'm doing my best to push them away. Because I just can't risk getting hurt."

Wendy pulled her in for a strong hug. "I understand everything you're feeling. All of it. You're not alone. And you're not crazy or weird or wrong."

"Thank you," Kassandra said, the tightness in her chest lifting.

"Do you want to come back to the table?"

"No." She laughed. "I think Brian is embarrassed, and I'm sorry for that."

"No, don't be. You were honest. No harm in that. I'm sorry we tried to set the two of you up. You told us not to, but we did it anyway. Can you forgive me?"

"Yes." Kassandra smiled as they pulled apart.

"Okay, go. I'll handle Brian. Call us, okay?"

Kassandra nodded and headed out to her car. The warm wind blew against her and she imagined more tiny pieces of her wall breaking off in it, settling behind her on the asphalt. She would go back to the kennel. She could handle Jayden. And she would let her friends in more.

She felt the best she'd felt in a long time.

CHAPTER TWENTY

Jayden pulled up on the car-lined street. She slowed her truck to a crawl and squinted in the dim light for a space to parallel park. As she searched she wondered for the hundredth time what she was doing there. Mel had insisted she come, somehow knowing her mind was on Kassandra all the time. Little did she know how right she was.

She backed into a space near one of her friends' vehicles. She'd see many of her friends here tonight, but she wasn't looking forward to it. She'd been to dozens of parties with her friends and she used to have fun. But lately they'd all been the same. Same women, just different couplings. Everyone was happily dating, having a good time, yet here she was second-guessing it all.

Was that really what she wanted from life? For this dating game to continue indefinitely? Why hadn't she settled down before? She'd met some really incredible women.

She locked her truck and headed up the sidewalk. The music was muffled, but she could still make out the song. "Love Shack" by the B-52s. It was an eighties-themed party, and she saw a few women ahead cross the road wearing miniskirts and ankle boots. Their bangs were high, and as she drew closer she could see the heavy makeup. Despite not really wanting to be there, it made her smile, and she just knew Mel would be wearing something crazy.

As for her own outfit, she was happy with her tight-fitting faded jeans, authentic pewter Vans shoes, and an old Vuarnet France T-shirt that fit her snugly. She even put on some Obsession for the evening.

"Hey, Jayden." A woman Jayden recognized welcomed her just inside the door. She couldn't remember her name, so she smiled and waved, heading farther inside the large house.

The music was now very loud, and people were laughing and shouting to be heard. A thick mass of women cluttered the living room, many of them dancing. Hugs began to come at her from people she knew but had a hard time recognizing with the makeup and hair. She returned the hugs and greetings and laughed at a few once she realized who they were. Everyone had gone all out in costume, and she was beginning to think she might have fun.

"Mel's out back," Deedee said, throwing her arm around her shoulders.

"Of course she is." Jayden knew exactly where Mel would be. And frankly, it was where she preferred to be as well.

Deedee gave her a squeeze and then stopped and turned her to face her. "You come alone?"

Jayden shrugged. "Yeah, I guess I did."

"I don't think I've ever seen you without a date."

"You have now." Jayden smiled.

"Well, damn. I think the earth just shook a little." Deedee patted her back and took a big swallow of beer. She was dressed in parachute pants and high-top Adidas shoes. Her shirt was torn and covered in safety pins.

"Speaking of which, where's your date?" Deedee and Maria had been together for over ten years.

Deedee looked around. "She's here somewhere. Last time I saw her she was chasing down a George Michael look-alike."

"Tell her I said hello." Jayden scanned the dozens of faces. Some she knew, some she knew she should know but couldn't quite tell. Others were just faces in a crowd. No one looked like Kassandra, and her heart sank at the realization. But then it lifted again as she let herself think about what Kassandra would be wearing if she were at the party.

"You okay, hot stuff?" Deedee asked.

Jayden couldn't look at her. "Yes. I was just looking for someone." She gave her a firm hug. "I better go find Mel."

Deedee winked at her and returned to the dancing crowd, beer held high.

Jayden wove her way through the wall of people and found the arcadia door. She slid it open and stepped back into the mild night. Chili pepper lights lined the top of the patio. Chimeneas burned in various corners of the yard, accompanied by lit hurricane lamps spread throughout the area for low lighting. The mood was very intimate, and Jayden felt her throat tighten as she once again thought of Kassandra.

The small pool was off to the left, the pool light changing colors every minute or so. Women lingered near the edges, talking, laughing. A few were in the pool, calling the others to come in. Jayden walked past them to the far corner of the yard, edging a couple of queen palms as she did so. She let out a whistle as she waited near a chimenea. She tossed in another piece of wood and stared at the firelight as she waited. Soon she heard rustling and soft cursing as Mel stepped out of the darkness.

" 'Bout time you showed," she said, wiping the corners of her black lips. She was dressed as Jayden had expected. New wave with late punk influence. Hair in a Mohawk-type style, heavy eye makeup that flared to her temples, pink, green, purple, long earrings, various chokers, and a black fishnet half top over a red bra.

"Nice boots," Jayden said, recognizing the old pair of Doc Martens leading up to black leather pants.

"You look…" Mel paused, looking her up and down, "Very mellow."

"Hey, I'm even wearing Obsession," Jayden said, defending herself.

"You're such a Goody Two-shoes."

"Right. We know both know that's not true."

More rustling came from behind the palms, and a woman in a tight-fitting minidress came out, looking perplexed.

"Are you coming back?" she asked, looking to Mel.

Mel took her hand. "Sure am. This is my friend Jayden. Jayden, this is Carly."

Jayden gave her a wave and resisted rolling her eyes. Mel had probably known her all of ten minutes.

"Hey, someone here is looking for you," Mel said with a wink.

"Oh God, who?" If Mel was excited, it couldn't be a good thing.

Mel snapped her fingers, obviously trying to remember a name. "Nora," she finally said. "From dinner a while back. She recognized me and remembered you."

Jayden had to think a moment. "Oh."

"Yeah, oh. She's here and I told her you were coming. She's disappointed that you haven't called."

Jayden sank her hands into her pockets. "Great, wonderful."

"Go grab a beer and see if you can find her. Bring her and join us." Mel playfully slapped her arm. "You might as well enjoy yourself while you're here."

Jayden stared into the firelight. She contemplated just

leaving and not dealing with any of it. But what would she do? Go home and pine over Kassandra? She knew she couldn't wish a woman to be interested, but she'd honestly never been in this position before. She didn't fall for straight women. Or women who were afraid to be interested.

"Hey, look. I know you're thinking about her, but come on, Jay, she's not here. She's at home reading or loving up on her boyfriend. Or whatever straight women do."

Jayden pushed out a sigh. "Yeah."

"Yeah?" Mel gripped her forearm in reassurance.

"Yeah." Jayden nodded and gave in. Mel was right. She should enjoy herself and push Kassandra out of her mind.

"That's my girl." Mel smiled. "Go grab a beer."

She led Carly back behind the palm trees to their secret spot.

Jayden went for the cooler on the patio. The music from the house rocked, and she hummed along to "You Make My Dreams" by Hall and Oates. She cracked open a bottle and took a few good sips of Miller Lite. The night was perfect, mid-seventies and clear skies. She closed her eyes and pushed all thoughts away. Her staff was covering all calls, giving her a much-needed night off. Another one of Mel's demands. But this time even Allie had agreed.

"Jayden, hey," Maria said, hurrying up to her. She tugged on a young George Michael. "Doesn't she look great?"

"Yes, she does."

The young woman had the aviator shades, leather bomber jacket, torn jeans, even the five o'clock shadow.

Maria hugged Jayden fiercely and kissed her cheeks. She was wearing leggings with leg warmers and Reebok high-tops. An off-the-shoulder half top showed off a neon sports bra.

"Deedee said you were here alone. I didn't believe her."

"I am."

Maria looked concerned. "What gives?"

"Nothing, I just don't have a date."

"Something's up. I know it." Maria held her chin and looked into her eyes. "Oh yes, something's different."

Jayden tried to pull away. "Nothing is up."

But Maria held firm. "Oh my God, Jayden, you're in love."

This time Jayden did pull away. She felt herself anger a little. "I'm fine."

"Jayden, Jesus." Maria whispered something to George Michael, causing her to leave them alone.

"Maria, I'm not in love. Nothing is up. I'm fine."

"Jayden Beaumont, how long have you known me?"

"Ten years."

"And in ten years have you ever known me to be wrong about you?"

Jayden looked away. Maria had never been wrong. It unnerved her sometimes being friends with someone who could read her so easily. Maria was gifted in ways she didn't quite understand. She was an empath and had the ability to feel and sense other people's feelings.

"She must be very special." Maria touched her hand.

Jayden's heart pounded and her throat felt like it was going to seize up. "I gotta go." She fished in the cooler for another beer.

Maria placed her hand on her shoulder. "If you want to talk about it, I'm here."

Jayden stood very still. Then she nodded and walked away.

She breathed deeply, pushing the words away. She wasn't about to let the words sink further in. She wasn't in love. How ridiculous. She just had an interest. And even the interest was ridiculous. It could go nowhere. It *would* go nowhere.

She needed to let it go.

She pushed past the palms and found Mel and Carly locked in an embrace, slow dancing to Phil Collins. A chimenea burned in the center of several lawn chairs. Jayden took a seat and finished her first beer. She pretended she didn't see her hand tremble.

"We're going to the bathroom," Mel announced. "Want anything?"

Jayden shook her head and eased back in the chair. She opened her second beer and took hearty sips. She stared at the scattering of a few distant stars. She needed to be alone. She needed a woman. She needed something. Anything. She just knew she had to stop Maria's words.

She ignored the rustling when she heard it, assuming it was Mel or Carly. But to her surprise, a woman walked through wearing a skintight little red dress. Her hair was thick and dark, her skin tanned and shimmering.

Jayden stood. It was Nora.

"Nice place you got here," she said, walking up to give her a lingering kiss on the cheek.

Jayden closed her eyes and inhaled her scent. It was Colors, a scent she hadn't smelled in a very long time.

"You're trembling," she said into her ear. "Is that because of me?"

Jayden swallowed the lump in her throat.

What perfume did Kassandra wear? She always smelled of lavender; even her home had smelled that way. Jayden loved it.

She gripped her beer and pushed the thought away.

"Mmm," she let out, too confused to speak.

Nora held her face with both warm hands and stared into her. Then she smiled coyly and leaned in for a soft, wet kiss.

Jayden froze, surprised. She thought of Kassandra and

Kassandra's lips. She dropped her beer and wrapped her arms around her, holding her close. She kissed her back and let her mind go. It went straight for Kassandra and exploded with sensation. Jayden gripped her ass and backed her to the wall. She plunged her tongue in her mouth and then slowed, imagining she was with Kassandra. She kissed her passionately, long and lingering, deep and sensual. Nora clawed her back through her T-shirt and pulled her mouth away. Both of them were panting with desire.

"You're making me so wet."

Jayden went for her neck, nibbling and kissing. She lowered her hand and traced her fingers up her thigh. She found her warm, her panties moist. Nora groaned and told her yes. Begged with please.

To Jayden, it was Kassandra calling to her, begging for her touch, for sweet release.

Jayden met her mouth again and conquered her as she slipped her hand into her underwear.

Nora let out a cry and clung to her as Jayden plunged inside her.

They rocked there together to "Total Eclipse of the Heart." Jayden with her eyes clenched, dreaming of Kassandra. Fucking Kassandra, licking her neck, biting her just behind the ear.

Nora moaned loud and then muffled as they collapsed for another kiss. When she came, she did so with vocal cries into the night. Jayden fucked her hard and strong, making sure she went to heaven and above. She let out a cry herself, knowing it wasn't Kassandra and knowing it was cutting her deeply. When they stilled, she gently pulled away from her and pushed her way out of the palms.

A small group was standing nearby, including Mel, who looked shocked and ashen. Some of the women clapped.

Jayden felt tears sting her eyes. Mel mouthed "I'm sorry" and looked to her left.

Jayden's eyes fell upon a blonde in a denim miniskirt and light pink sweater. Despite her makeup, Jayden nearly jerked as she recognized Kassandra.

"Kassandra?" What was she doing there? Jayden shook her head in disbelief.

Kassandra looked shell-shocked and torn apart. She looked straight at Jayden and then at Nora, who came up from behind, wrapping her arms around her and kissing her neck.

Jayden stepped away, stepped toward Kassandra, but Kassandra gave her the most pain-filled look she'd ever seen and then turned and ran through the crowd.

Jayden went to go after her, but a woman she didn't know stopped her, holding her by the arm.

Jayden tried to jerk away, but the woman held fierce. "Let her go," she said softly. "My wife went after her. She'll be okay."

Jayden needed to see her, needed to explain. This couldn't be happening.

"I need to talk to her."

"I think right now it's pretty safe to say you're the last person she wants to talk to."

Jayden yanked her arm away and Mel came to stand by her side.

"I'm asking you nicely to leave her alone," the woman said.

"Who are you?" Mel asked.

"I'm Kassandra's best friend."

"Yeah, well I'm *her* best friend," Mel said, motioning to Jayden.

"And who are you, exactly?" the woman asked.

Jayden was still staring after Kassandra, hoping she'd see her reemerge from the crowd.

"Jayden," Jayden said softly.

"Wait a minute, you're the dog shelter woman, aren't you?"

"Yes."

"I didn't know she was here, Jay. I swear," Mel said. "What the hell was she doing here anyway?"

"She came with my wife and me. She's our friend."

Mel squeezed Jayden's hand, but Jayden pulled away. She didn't want to be touched. She felt dirty.

"Does she know it's a lesbian party?" Mel asked, still sounding pissed. "Didn't you warn her that women would be kissing and touching and whatever?"

"My friend is not an idiot."

"Then why did she freak out?"

The woman followed Jayden's gaze. "That's the big question, isn't it?"

Jayden walked into the house and wove between people. She headed out the front door just in time to see Kassandra's car drive away. A woman stood on the sidewalk hugging herself. Jayden trotted down the steps and fished out her car keys.

The woman spotted her. "What did you do to her?"

Jayden stopped. "Are you talking to me?"

The woman approached, her face sad and concerned. "What did you do to her? Have you been having an affair with her?"

"No. I haven't done anything."

"She's never been with a woman, you know."

"I didn't do anything."

"Who are you?"

Jayden grew angry. She just wanted to get to Kassandra.

"Jayden. I already spoke to your wife."

"Well, Jayden, my friend is very upset."

"Yeah, well, so am I." She stepped around her and walked quickly to her truck. She threw open the door and climbed inside. She stared at her cell phone, wanting to call Kassandra. But she didn't know what she would say. What she should say. What exactly had she done wrong? And why had Kassandra looked so hurt? Had she been right from the start?

Did she just totally fucking blow it?

Jayden shut her door and cranked her engine. She drove away chasing Kassandra, having no idea where she went. But for now, anywhere sounded better than where she was.

CHAPTER TWENTY-ONE

Kassandra awoke to Lula standing on her chest, giving her kisses on the mouth.

"All right, all right." She rubbed her head and Lula jumped down and barked with excitement. Kassandra slid her feet into her slippers and walked into the front room for the leash. It was seven o'clock and she was still half dead. Sleep hadn't come easily the night before, and it pained her to remember why.

"Come on," she encouraged her with a high-pitched voice. Lula sat while Kassandra put on her leash. Kassandra turned off the door alert, unlocked it, and stepped outside. The morning was cool but not crisp, and she stood in the grass in her pajamas, too tired to care who saw. Lula did her business and they returned inside. Kassandra then went for the coffeemaker and settled down on the couch. Her cell phone sat on the coffee table. She'd purposely left it out of her room.

She knew there were texts and messages. They'd been calling since she'd left the party. She just hadn't felt like talking. She'd been so torn up and somehow devastated that she'd barely made it home in one piece. And she still didn't know why she was so upset.

Of course Jayden had someone. Of course she was dating

and having sex. She was a healthy woman. Why wouldn't she be?

But yet, the sight of her with that woman had nearly killed her. And the noises they'd been making in the dark corner. It had ripped her open and left her guts all over that yard.

She closed her eyes as the pain came again. Jayden was with someone. Taken. She wasn't into her, despite what she'd said or done. Or maybe she was and she'd just wanted a fling.

Either way brought pain. But she would be fine. She would get through it, because it only proved her reasons for not dating in the first place. It was easier to stay alone, to not deal with people and emotions and promises and lies and everything else.

She felt stronger now. More in control. Jayden was out, gone from her mind. Her silly staring could stop, her silly fantasizing.

She unplugged her phone and scrolled through the messages. Her friends were, of course, worried. A few other people she knew from the party had also texted her asking her if she was okay. She put the phone on speaker and listened to her three voice messages. Two were from Katelynn and Wendy, asking her to call them today, and one was just silence. She deleted the messages and checked her missed calls. Jayden Beaumont had called at 12:27 a.m.

Kassandra touched her name. Jayden had called her soon after she'd left. What did it mean? She recalled Jayden's face and remembered that it had looked pained as well. She looked to be upset before the shock of seeing her had appeared.

Kassandra eyed her number. She was tempted to call.

Lula jumped onto the couch and settled in her lap. She wouldn't have Lula if it weren't for Jayden.

She groaned. "Oh God, why has this woman gotten to me?" She rose and went for coffee. She felt so stupid now after the whole thing. Someone says a few flattering words to her and she's head over heels, only to be made a fool of. And off she'd run, like a crying schoolgirl upset over her first crush.

She sipped her coffee and steeled herself. Despite her best efforts, she was still an emotional creature. She was still sensitive and easily hurt. She put up her walls, but she hadn't stuck to them. How much longer would she let this go on? She eased back onto the couch and thought back to her father and all the times he'd broken promises. He'd eventually stopped with the promises and stopped with talking to her altogether. She'd spent time and money on therapy, knowing she still had issues with this, and with loving him despite his behavior. She'd done the same with her husband. Loved him despite the way he'd treated her. She'd just kept taking it, believing the lies and promises. Hoping he would change. But he never did, and neither did her father.

What made her think that people could change now? That Jayden could somehow mean what she'd said that first day?

She was a fool, once again.

Lula settled back into her lap, and she scratched her and said with determination, "Not anymore. Not anymore."

CHAPTER TWENTY-TWO

"Boys, bring those boards over here," Jayden said, straightening to wipe the light sweat from her brow. The boys were helping her repair the steps to her front porch. It wasn't an urgent job, and truthfully, it had been done a few years ago along with the whole porch, but she couldn't stand sun rot and she needed something to do with her hands.

"You think she's ever coming back?" Gus asked, nailing a board in place. Billy returned from the truck with a stack of boards. He knelt and let them fall to the ground.

"Nah, man, she's busy. She's like a really good person. She's got important things to do."

"Aren't we important?"

Jayden took a swig of lukewarm water. "Of course you're important, and it has nothing to do with you."

"So why isn't she here?"

Jayden took a board and handed it to Gus, then helped him line it up. "It's my fault she isn't here. You guys didn't do anything. She still cares about you." She hated seeing them hurt and worry over the situation. She'd considered calling Kassandra again and again, but she really had no idea what to say.

"What did you do, Beaumont?"

Jayden handed Gus the nail gun. The boys loved using the nail gun. It was the main reason why they were so eager to help her with the steps.

"It was a misunderstanding."

"What kind of misunderstanding?"

"An adult misunderstanding." She didn't know how else to explain it, not even to herself.

"Did you hurt her? Because that would piss me off."

Jayden looked him square in the eye. "I would never intentionally hurt her."

"So you unintentionally hurt her?" Billy asked, holding out his hand for the nail gun.

Jayden considered her answer. Both boys were looking at her, and she never lied to them. Ever.

"Yes, I think I did."

They looked at one another and continued nailing.

"Did you apologize?" Billy asked, holding his hand out for another board. Jayden grabbed one and gave it to him.

"I tried to."

"'I'm sorry' is always a good place to start," Gus said. "Shit, Beaumont, even I know that."

"Yeah," Billy said. "You should call her. Like now."

"I'll handle it, guys, don't worry." But would she? Did she have the guts to call at this point? Now it just seemed hopeless.

Gus stood and wiped the sweat from his forehead with his bandanna. He went for the water cooler and turned back to them. "Looks like you won't need to call."

Jayden looked over at him. "What?"

He smiled. "She's here."

Jayden and Billy stood, shading their brows in the November sun.

Kassandra was walking toward them, snug San Francisco baseball cap on her head. Jayden couldn't help but scan her body. She wore a tight-fitting green tee and short khaki shorts. Jayden could smell the lavender scent on her from a few feet away.

"Hi, guys," she said with a smile.

Jayden's heart tripped over itself.

"Just 'hi, guys'?" Gus said. "That's all you say to us after disappearing?"

Her smile fell. "I—"

Gus grinned and hugged her. "I'm just messing with you. Glad to have you back."

"Yeah, it's good to see you, Ms. H.," Billy said. "We missed you, right, Beaumont?" All eyes fell to Jayden.

"Right." Jayden smiled and met Kassandra's gaze briefly. They both looked at the boys.

"We're fixing the porch," Gus said.

Kassandra examined the work so far. "Looks good."

"They're pretty good with their hands," Jayden said, kneeling alongside them to continue. Most of the boards were in place. She showed them what to do with the remaining boards and stood again, sliding her hands into her back pockets.

"You guys good to finish up?" she asked.

"Yep. We got it."

Jayden turned to Kassandra. "Can I talk to you for just a moment?"

Kassandra looked panicked for the briefest of moments, and Jayden's heart sank. But she seemed to recover quickly. "Sure."

"Great."

Jayden led the way inside her home, stepping up on the porch next to the rebuilt steps. She turned and offered Kassandra a hand. Kassandra took it and stepped up as well, dropping her hand and thanking her.

"It's quiet inside," Jayden said, opening the door to let her in. Jayden closed the door behind them and calmed her dogs as they came to say hello.

Kassandra loved on each of them, and Jayden started in, nervous as hell. "I just wanted to say thanks," she said, letting out a deep breath.

"For what?" Kassandra asked, turning to look at her.

"For coming back."

Kassandra picked up Louie, a small terrier mix. "Oh, no problem."

Jayden still felt nervous, and Kassandra's calm demeanor only made it worse. "Are you okay? I mean, are we okay?"

Kassandra kissed Louie and hugged him close to her chin. "Yeah. We're good."

Jayden wiped her sweaty palms on her shorts. "Good, because you know I'm sorry about what happened and everything."

"Sorry about what? You have nothing to be sorry about."

"But you—"

"I just freaked is all. And I have so many other things on my mind. I think I just lost it all at once."

Jayden squirmed. Kassandra was one tough cookie to crack. She thought about dropping it, but she didn't like unfinished business. You had to get the whole splinter out or it would fester and get infected. Better to just dig in and get it all out.

"I just wanted you to know that...I'm not going to act on my feelings for you. As far as I'm concerned, we're friends. But I meant what I said. I'm not going anywhere. I'm here for you. In whatever sense that means."

Kassandra's eyes watered and she looked away quickly. "Thank you."

"I understand that it was a mistake. Things got a little carried away. I should've stopped it. But I—"

"Was it?" Kassandra asked. "A mistake?"

Jayden fought for words. "I thought that you thought it was."

"It didn't feel like a mistake."

Jayden flushed.

"It felt good, passionate."

Jayden moved to the fridge where she retrieved two water bottles. She was suddenly very hot. "You thirsty?" She handed one over, but Kassandra didn't take it. She was still staring at her.

"I don't want to deny what it was," Kassandra said. "I just don't think I can handle it is all."

A barking sound started, and Jayden looked desperately from dog to dog, needing to make it stop.

"I think it's your phone," Kassandra said.

Jayden felt her hip. "Damn." She answered quickly. "Beaumont."

She turned and plugged her other ear, the caller difficult to hear.

"Jayden. I just got a call. Two kids riding dirt bikes saw a dog trapped on the second story of an old farmhouse. I'm stuck on another call. You want it?"

"Of course." Jayden hurried to the counter and took down directions. She ended the call and returned the phone to her hip. "I've got to go. There's a dog in need out past Avondale." She dug in her fridge for more water bottles, placing them all in a cooler. Then she grabbed her emergency bag for the dogs, which she always kept stocked and ready and near the door. "Shit." She stopped in her tracks. "Mel's in Tucson."

She looked at Kassandra. "I need you to go with me. I need you to hold the ladder for me."

Kassandra set Louie back on the floor. "Okay."

"Can you handle it? The dog is probably in bad shape."

"Yes."

Jayden grabbed the bag and the cooler and crossed the porch to jump off the edge. She loaded the truck and retrieved the ladder from behind the house. Gus helped her tie it down in the bed of the truck.

"Can we go?" he asked as he saw Kassandra climbing in the passenger side.

"I need you here," Jayden said. "Finish the steps and then help Allie. We're a person short today, so I'm counting on you guys."

"You got it, Beaumont," Billy said. "Hey, did you tell her you're sorry?"

Jayden nodded and he smiled.

She slid in behind the wheel, started the engine, and took off.

❖

Jayden relayed the details to Kassandra as they sped down I-17 to the 101 loop, which would take them to the southwest valley.

"So the dog is trapped on the second floor of an old house," Kassandra said, tugging on her hat.

"Yes. The bikers said she's alive and that they couldn't reach her because the stairs were unstable and they didn't have a ladder. The good news is she's alive and out of the sun. The bad news is we don't know how long she's been there or what her condition is."

"Right. Shouldn't we call someone else for help, though? Like maybe the fire department?"

Jayden thought about it, but she knew the terrain was rough and it might be something she could do herself.

"Let's wait and see."

They rode in silence, save for Jayden calling Allie to give her the information. Jayden was in work mode now. Rescue mode. All she could think about was getting to that dog. From time to time she looked over at Kassandra, who was content watching the road. Jayden thought about polite conversation, but with what they'd just talked about, she wasn't sure what to say.

"Here we go," Jayden finally said as she pulled off and headed west toward the sun. "She's somewhere off one of these trails." They were in desert now, between developments. "There's the rock place," Jayden said, turning on her signal. The trail was across from the landscaping rock supply company. "There!"

She turned onto the dirt trail and accelerated a little, taking it as quickly but as carefully as she could. They rode for about ten minutes before Kassandra spotted the old house off to the left. Jayden turned and took it slow, completely off trail now. She could see tracks from dirt bikes in the dirt.

"How old do you think that is?" Kassandra asked as they approached.

"I have no idea. It's hard to tell with the weather and rot the sun causes."

She came to a stop and put the truck in park. She and Kassandra climbed out and they walked to the front of the house. The windows were gone, the boards old and weathered, with a room on the left collapsed in by the rotten roof.

"She must be over here," Jayden said, heading for the right of the house. They rounded the corner and got a straight shot into the second story. The boards from the house had fallen away, and some of the roof had come down. It was where they saw her and then heard her.

"There she is," Kassandra said, pointing.

The little white dog was lying on her side. She tried to

move when she heard them, but her hind leg seemed to be caught on something. She whined loudly.

"Well, that's a good sign," Jayden said. "She's still got some life in her."

She moved to the truck and Kassandra followed, helping her with the ladder. Jayden placed it as close to the house as she could.

"You sure we shouldn't wait for the fire department?" Kassandra asked, touching her arm just before she placed her foot on the bottom step of the ladder.

Jayden looked at her hand, then at her. She saw concern, and it warmed her heart. "I'm hoping I won't have to step inside the house. I'm hoping I can free her from the ladder."

Kassandra looked up at the dog. "Okay."

"Support me, and hopefully, we'll have her out of there in no time."

Kassandra held the ladder as Jayden climbed.

"Thanks, that's good. I feel secure." She was level with the dog and she leaned over to take a look at her leg. The dog got excited and tried to move, only causing more pain. "Shh, easy, girl. I'm right here." She reached out and stroked her head. The dog relaxed and lay back down. Jayden stepped up another rung and leaned in more. She fingered the bind that was knotted around the dog's leg. It was a wad of neon, some sort of binding material.

"What is it? Is it rope?"

"No. It's something else," Jayden called down. "I'm going to try to cut it." She fished out her knife and passed it to her left hand. She leaned in again, balancing carefully. She placed the blade under an area away from the dog. It wouldn't free the dog from the bind, but it would free the dog from the house.

She pulled upward and cut. The dog let out a yip but moved its free leg immediately.

"Got it." She slid her knife back in her pocket and stroked the dog, who was now standing but trembling. "Come here, baby." She let go of the ladder to grab her with both hands. Once she was secure and had her tucked with one arm against her chest, she started down the ladder.

"Be careful," Kassandra said.

Jayden took four steps down and the dog started squirming. "Shh, it's okay, it's okay." But the dog was frightened, and she was fighting to get free. Kassandra was calling up to her, and Jayden was trying with all her might to hold the dog close. She stepped down again and lost her footing, throwing her balance off. Kassandra screamed as Jayden fell. She clenched her eyes and held the dog tightly. When she hit, it made a horrible thump and she couldn't breathe.

Kassandra was over her, touching her face. "Can you hear me? Jayden?"

Jayden held out the dog, who was safe on her chest. "Take her," was all she could manage to say. She fought for breath, but everything felt tight in her back and chest. She rolled to her side and the pain registered.

"Ah, fuck." Her back and head were killing her. She regained her breathing and felt behind her to make sure nothing was in her back. She heard the truck door slam and Kassandra was back at her side, phone to her ear.

"Yes, I need an ambulance," she said. "Please hurry. She's fallen from a second story." Kassandra pressed on her shoulder, making her lie flat on her back. "Don't move," she said.

Jayden tried to sit up, but Kassandra forced her down. "Don't move or I'll kick your ass."

Jayden stilled. The look in Kassandra's eye was serious, one she didn't want to mess with.

"Where's the dog?" Jayden asked.

Kassandra was speaking to 911. She covered the phone and said, "In the truck. She's fine."

"Take care of her."

"I will. But right now, I'm taking care of you."

"Hang up and call my friend Oliver at the emergency vet clinic. He owes me a favor. He'll come get her."

"Jayden, shut up." Kassandra pressed her fingers to her lips. When she quieted, Kassandra held her hand and kept speaking into the phone. She was calm and cool. Yet firm. She even argued with the operator. "I don't care what you have to send, just get here. She hit her head, she's bleeding. Just get here, damn it!"

"I'm bleeding?" Jayden couldn't tell. "Where am I bleeding?"

Kassandra squeezed her hand. "It's okay. You've got a cut on your head." Jayden tried to raise her arm to feel for it, but Kassandra wouldn't let her.

"I'm setting the phone down now," Kassandra said to the operator. "I'm putting you on speaker. I need to talk to Jayden."

"Jayden, how are you feeling? Do you hurt?" she asked gently while sweeping her hair back from her forehead. Jayden looked into her eyes and felt like getting lost in them.

"My head," she said. "My back."

"Okay, anywhere else?"

"No."

"They are sending a chopper for you. Just hang on. Can you squeeze my fingers?"

Jayden did.

"Good, now how about with this hand?"

Jayden did.

"Good. Now can you feel this?" She lightly touched her legs. It gave her goose flesh and quickened her breath.

"Yes."

Kassandra smiled. "Very good. They are going to take you in the helicopter, and I'm going to drop the dog off at the emergency clinic. Then I'll come to the hospital, okay?"

"Yeah," Jayden said, throat growing dry.

"Is she still conscious?" the operator asked.

"Yes, she is. She's coherent and talking."

"The air evac is en route. You should see them any minute now."

"You're coming to the hospital?" Jayden asked.

"Yes."

"Good."

"Is that good?"

"Yes. I'm afraid of needles."

Kassandra laughed playfully. "I would've never guessed."

"I don't go around telling people."

"But with the dogs and all you deal with…"

"As long as it isn't me, I'm fine."

Kassandra nodded and squeezed her hand again. "I'll hold your hand, okay?"

Jayden smiled. She felt nauseous. "I need to throw up."

"Hang on, I hear them now." She looked away and Jayden heard the helicopter approach.

Black floaters came into her vision. Jayden clung to her hand. She called her name.

"I'm here," Kassandra said.

"I need you to know," Jayden said.

"Shh, okay," Kassandra said, touching her forehead again.

"I want to be with you."

Kassandra palmed her cheek. Jayden swallowed and fought off the waning vision.

"Did you hear me?" She had to be sure that she heard.

"Yes, I heard you."

Jayden closed her eyes. "Okay. I'm glad."

Around her she heard people clamoring, talking, unwrapping things. When she felt the prick in her arm, she let it all go and let the blackness take over.

Chapter Twenty-three

Kassandra watched the helicopter lift off. She stared after it for a long moment before climbing in the truck and adjusting the seat. The dog, who was eager to see her, came to her, and she soothed her and told her it would be okay. She limped and panted, and Kassandra held her close as she drove out of the desert and back onto the paved road. She headed south to Peoria and then drove quickly to the emergency clinic. She'd already called Allie and reported everything, and Allie had said she would call the animal clinic for her.

When she arrived, she carried the little dog inside and they took her with eager hands, all of them wishing Jayden well.

Kassandra made them promise to call her with an update on the dog. Then she got back into the truck and sped to the hospital. Her hands trembled, but not with fear. She was still in a little bit of shock over what had happened. Seeing Jayden fall had been horrifying, and seeing her hurt and helpless had torn her apart. She had to make sure she was okay.

Her words only intensified her feelings, making her drive faster. Jayden wanted her. Could it be true? As thrilled as she felt over it, it only confused her all the more. Could she let her in? It was all she'd been thinking about. But in coming back to the kennel, she'd accepted that they must be friends. Even

Jayden had said so. Faced with an emergency, though, she'd confessed otherwise. She'd confessed what they both felt.

She pulled into the emergency lot and parked, then ran inside the ER and asked for Jayden's whereabouts.

"Are you family?"

She hesitated. "No."

"One moment, please."

Kassandra paced.

"Name?"

"Kassandra Haden. I'm her friend and coworker. Please, I need to know how she is."

From a distant curtain, a woman was arguing, voice raised, insisting on leaving. Kassandra stood on her toes and tried to see around the corner.

"That's her, that's my friend. Can I please go see her?"

The woman looked behind her at the rising commotion. A man in scrubs hurried from behind the curtain, shaking his head. He tore off his surgical gloves and stopped at the counter to make notes in a chart.

"Is that the air evac in curtain five?" the woman asked.

He didn't look up from his scribble. "Yes. But I don't recommend going in there. She's combative."

Kassandra spoke up. "Can I go? Please? I might be able to calm her down. I'm her friend."

He finally stopped his hand and looked up. "We're giving her a sedative. So she may be a little loopy."

"I understand."

"Does she have family here?"

"She doesn't have...family."

"I see." He closed the chart. "Come with me."

Kassandra rounded the counter and followed him as he pulled back the curtain and entered. He approached the head of the bed on one side and Kassandra did the same on the other. Jayden looked at her with wild eyes, IV in her hand, wrists strapped to the bed.

"Tell them to let me go," she said.

Kassandra looked to the doctor, who cleared his throat to talk.

"Ms. Beaumont, is it all right if I speak freely in front of your friend here?"

Jayden tugged at the straps. "Yes, fine. I don't care. Just let me go."

"As soon as you relax we can undo the straps. But in the meantime, we need you to remain still with the IV in your hand."

Jayden closed her mouth and flexed her jaw. A bandage was on her temple near her scalp. Blood had seeped through. Loose grass clung to her hair. She shifted, showing bare legs and a light blue hospital gown. She groaned.

"You'll be in some pain for a couple of weeks," the doctor said. "But the good news is, you have no broken bones and your CAT scan showed no serious damage. You do have a concussion, so we'd like to keep you awake and under observation until tomorrow."

"What about her back?" Kassandra asked.

"X-rays looked good. She's scraped up and she'll have some killer bruises. And like I said, she'll be really sore. But she should be fine in a few weeks. I'll recommend a physical therapist in case she feels she needs it."

"I won't need it," Jayden said. "I'll be fine."

The doctor sighed as if he'd tried to have this conversation with her before Kassandra's arrival. "Ms. Beaumont, you've suffered a serious fall here. You're going to be forced to take it easy while you heal. You'll be very stiff and sore."

"I don't have time to take it easy," she said. "I have a kennel to run. Dogs to care for. Teens to look after."

He looked to Kassandra. "I'm afraid you're going to have to ask for help as far as that goes."

"She has it," Kassandra said. "She just doesn't utilize it."

Jayden narrowed her eyes at her. "Kassandra, you're not helping here."

"Make sure that she does," the doctor said. He reached down and squeezed Jayden's hand. "I need you to follow up with your family physician next week, okay? She can manage your pain and continued care."

He then reached across and shook Kassandra's hand. "Keep a close eye on her."

"I will, thank you."

He nodded and whisked out through the closed curtain. Kassandra pulled up a chair and settled in.

"How are you feeling?" She carefully began pulling the grass from her hair.

"Angry."

"Besides that."

The scowl on her face slowly began to fade and she blinked long and slow. Kassandra held her hand. "There you go, just breathe deep and relax."

"I don't…like the needle in my hand."

"I know, but it needs to stay. Just relax and don't think about it."

Her breathing began to slow, and a smile curled her lips. "They cut my clothes off. Ruined my favorite pair of cargo shorts. Fuckers."

Kassandra laughed. "They did what they had to."

Jayden closed her eyes and breathed deeply. "I feel good. Like I could float away."

"Don't do that. Stay with me. Talk to me."

She opened her eyes. "The dog."

"She's fine. I'm waiting for an update, but she was very

alert and responsive on the way to the clinic. And Allie is taking care of everything at the kennel."

Jayden squeezed her hands. "I have so much to do. I've got to help the boys finish the steps—"

"Not right now you don't. Right now, you need to relax and heal."

"I can't," she said. A tear slipped down her face. "I have so much to do."

Kassandra squeezed her hand in return. "Jayden. You have to let go. Let the others help. I'm here. I'm going to help."

Her eyes shifted to her. "You will?"

"Of course."

"I…never know with you. I seem to chase you away."

A heavy feeling of guilt washed over Kassandra. "I'm here now," was all she could think to say.

"Good, because I need you."

Kassandra studied her closely. She knew the sedative had kicked in and Jayden's walls were down. But still the confession surprised her, and even more than that…moved her. She didn't think Jayden was the type to ever need anyone. But maybe that was her shield. Maybe she used that attitude to protect herself like she did.

"You do?" Kassandra asked softly.

"Yes." She licked her dry lips. "You make everything… right. You make it all fit, like a puzzle that was missing a piece."

Kassandra felt her breath catch. She held her hand, felt Jayden stroke her with her thumb.

"Don't leave again," she said. "No matter how afraid you are."

"How do you know I'm afraid?"

"Because I am."

Kassandra looked away, her eyes too deep, too penetrating.

"I just…" She swallowed against a burning throat. "I…people fail me. My father made promises he never kept. I know it shouldn't, but it still sticks with me. People don't do what they say or say what they mean. And I'm…left all alone…waiting for them to follow through."

"I get it," Jayden said. "The teens, they feel the same way. Maybe that's why you're so good with them."

"Maybe."

"Kassandra?"

Kassandra met her heavy gaze.

"Like I said before. I'm not going anywhere. I'll be here. In whatever way you need."

Kassandra took a deep, shaky breath, the tears rising and frustrating her. "Okay."

"No, I mean it. I won't disappear. I'm here."

Kassandra laughed a little to break the heaviness.

"No, I mean it."

The curtain rings scraped and Kassandra turned to find Mel entering, face ashen, eyes wide with concern.

"What the hell happened? Are you okay?" She rushed to Jayden's side. "Allie said you fell."

"I'm fine, I'm fine. Just a little banged up."

"You look like hell."

Kassandra stood, knowing that was her cue to go. Jayden looked at her while Mel continued on.

"Don't go," she finally said.

"I need to get back. Check on the dog." She knew Jayden wouldn't argue with that.

"I'll see you soon."

Mel unstrapped her wrists, cursing softly.

"Be careful. She tries to pull her IV out," Kassandra said.

Mel shot her a look. "Yeah, I got it. You can go."

Kassandra burned at her tone but said nothing. Jayden

needed to rest, and she knew Mel would take care of her. She waved and quietly walked out. Jayden's eyes were wide and full. But she couldn't stay, not even if Mel left. Jayden was opening her up, filling her with kindness and understanding, offering to be there, no matter what. With the exception of Katelynn and Wendy, no one had ever followed through on that. She reminded herself of that as she walked into the setting sun, squinting against the light, squinting against Jayden's words that were trying their very best to penetrate. She slipped on her shades, battling back. Even if Jayden meant it, only time would allow her to prove it. And she just didn't know how much longer she could fend her off without crushing her lips to hers and getting lost in her soul.

CHAPTER TWENTY-FOUR

Jayden groaned and the dogs moved, allowing her to sit up on the couch. She scowled at Mel, who stood from the nearby chair to hand over the cane she'd bought for her.

"I told you, no cane."

Mel scoffed. "Jesus, will you cut it with the bravado. It helps you balance better in case your back tweaks."

Again, she waved it off and stood. "I'm fine. Better." She paused as a bolt of pain shot through her back muscles. "Every day."

"Mm-hmm." Mel tried to cup her elbow, but Jayden glared at her.

"I'm just going to the kitchen."

"Why? What do you need?"

She didn't answer, just moved carefully across the room, dogs walking slowly at her heels. She wanted to get the chilled wine from the fridge and set the table for Kassandra. She was due any minute with a homemade casserole. Jayden's mouth watered just thinking about it. The bean burritos Mel had been bringing her were good, but they were getting old, fast. She'd made the mistake of telling her that's what she was craving when she got home from the hospital. Mel had gone into overdrive, bringing her several from one of their favorite Mexican restaurants.

"What are you doing?" Mel asked as Jayden retrieved the wine and set it on the counter to open. She sighed as she pulled out the corkscrew. There was no way she could open it. Mel would have to do it.

"Will you open this?" She slid her the bottle.

"I see," she said. "Straight girl is coming over."

"She's bringing dinner, and her name is Kassandra."

"Her name is 'tease.'"

Jayden gave her a look, warning her. She didn't tolerate Mel berating Kassandra, and Mel knew it.

"Okay, okay." She grabbed the bottle and got to work with the corkscrew. "If you like her so much why don't you ask her to move in here with you while you heal?"

"Are you saying you've had enough of me?"

"No." She grunted as she twisted. "I'm saying this is the perfect opportunity to have her close. To get to know her better. To, you know, get her in your bed."

Jayden jerked and winced as the corked popped. "I'm not trying to seduce her, Mel."

"Why not?"

"Because she needs to feel how she feels. Figure things out on her own."

"You're chicken shit." Mel slid the bottle back to her and Jayden poured the wine into two glasses.

"You wish. I just really care about her, Mel. If she ends up wanting me, then she does. I'm not going to push it."

"How noble," Mel said. "As always. I just don't know how you have the patience when you have so many women who would gladly have you."

"I don't want them. And besides, I don't expect anything, so I'm never disappointed."

"How long will you wait, Jay?"

Jayden shrugged. "I might have these feelings for her

forever. Even if she only wants to remain friends. I'll just have to figure out how to move on. If I can. Right now, I can't even imagine another woman."

Mel shook her head. "You're too good for me, girl. Too good for me."

Jayden smiled. "Just wait, someday you'll feel like this."

"Right."

"You will. It will happen."

Mel gave a wave. "On that note, I will bid you good-bye. You want me back tonight?"

"Nah."

"Got it. Later, Romeo." She breezed out the door and Jayden carried the glasses to the table and began carefully readying it for dinner. It had been a week since the accident, and she was slowly coming around to feeling normal. Mel had temporarily moved in to help her get around, and for a while she'd needed it. But now she was feeling stronger, the pain was dulling, and she could move around better. Kassandra would be pleased.

She'd come by almost every day since the accident, bringing food, wine, playing with the dogs. Not to mention the work she'd done at the kennel. The teens were raving about her, and Allie was even impressed. Jayden had felt herself glow in her presence, even when she put her foot down and told Jayden to take it easy. She seemed to really care, and it felt nice. Right.

"Knock, knock," Kassandra said as she peeked around the cracked door.

Jayden turned carefully and smiled. "Come on in."

Kassandra greeted the dogs and stepped inside carrying a glass casserole dish covered in foil. "It's still warm," she said, smiling.

"I can already taste it," Jayden said.

"Did you tell her no more burritos?" She set the dish on the counter, removed the lid, and searched for a spoon.

"I don't have the heart. She really thinks I love them that much. Plus, Mel's not exactly creative that way. She thinks like your average straight dude."

"If that means she's anything like my ex-husband, then I completely understand."

Jayden tried to smile, but the mention of her ex-husband again made her stomach drop. The thought of someone having Kassandra and not appreciating how incredible she was infuriated her. Not to mention the thought of that person being a man. Was Kassandra still attracted to men? Would she ever accept her as a woman? Accept her attraction? They were questions that drove her mad when she allowed them. But like she'd told Mel, she was pushing them away and expecting nothing but a good friendship, and so far, Kassandra had been a great friend to have in her corner.

Kassandra helped her set the table, and they settled in as she scooped out chicken casserole for the both of them. The dogs all lay at the entrance to the dining area, having been trained not to enter when people were eating at the table. Seven dogs begging for food could be a little overwhelming.

"Mmm, great wine." Kassandra sipped heartily and Jayden tried not to notice how it stained her beautiful lips.

"I had Allie pick some up. Mel, well, I already explained about Mel."

"Right."

Jayden sipped hers lightly. She was still on a light dose of painkillers so she had to be careful with alcohol. She didn't want to get woozy in front of Kassandra because she honestly couldn't remember what she'd said to her the last time she was. She vaguely recalled telling her that she wanted her after she'd fallen. That confession alone made her uneasy, and she felt exposed. She wished she could remember Kassandra's response.

"How are you feeling?" Kassandra asked, blowing on a bite of food.

Jayden swallowed, thanking God that Kassandra knew how to cook. "Better every day."

"Still stiff?"

"Yes."

"I can help you stretch after dinner."

Jayden nearly dropped her fork. Mel helped her stretch twice a day. There was no way she could let Kassandra do it. She didn't trust herself not to heat and embarrass herself at the close proximity.

"Thanks, but Mel already did."

Kassandra looked down, and Jayden wasn't sure if she saw disappointment cross her face.

"I wish you'd let me do more for you," she said, forking another bite.

"You do plenty."

"I do a lot at the kennel, but here…I feel like you're careful with me somehow. Like you don't want me to get too close. I thought we were friends."

Jayden gulped her wine. "We are."

"Then let me help."

"I do."

Kassandra sighed. "How about your laundry? Has Mel done that?"

"I did. Today."

"Jayden, you shouldn't be doing that. Not yet."

Jayden warmed from the wine. She wanted another glass to help ease her growing anxiety, but she resisted. "I'm okay."

"What about your bedding?"

Jayden couldn't think quickly enough and Kassandra pounced.

"Good, I'll change that out for you."

Jayden tried to argue, but Kassandra gave her a look, warning her not to even think about it. Jayden didn't push.

"So, how are you? Things going well at school?"

Kassandra's face clouded. She tried to smile but failed. "I just keep thinking I'd be happier somewhere else. I love the kids, but I just feel like my hands are tied with them. I'm the librarian, not a counselor. I just can't seem to help them enough. And no one else seems interested in doing so."

Jayden chewed and shrugged. "So why don't you counsel?"

Kassandra looked up and blinked. "You mean change my profession?"

"Sure. If that's what makes you happy. Why not?"

"I don't know. I've never really put much thought into it. I guess I'd have to go back to school."

"Would that be a deal breaker?"

Kassandra played with her food. "No, not necessarily."

"I say do what makes you happy. I couldn't imagine working a job I didn't like." She was damn lucky she had her kennel. Working a nine-to-five in an office sound hellish to her. She needed to breathe the fresh air, even if it was 115 degrees. And she couldn't imagine not being able to work with the dogs. They gave her so much love and affection and filled almost every void deep inside. Almost every void.

Kassandra finally forked another bite. "I'll think about it." She smiled, and this time it reached her eyes. "Thanks."

Jayden loved seeing her happy. She desperately wanted to tell her she was trying to locate her student Tony, but she wanted it to be a surprise if she found him. She knew from her phone calls that he'd been put in the system, and Kassandra was always upset when she talked about it, feeling responsible. She missed Tony at the school. His presence seemed to be the only thing she looked forward to at work anymore. Jayden wished she could make it all better, but there was only so much she could do.

She tried her best not to stare at her as they finished eating. She still felt a little light-headed from the wine, and Kassandra had a second glass. They talked about the teens as they rose and walked the dishes to the sink. Kassandra insisted on cleaning up, and Jayden argued but only halfheartedly. She was growing tired and weak, and she tried her best not to show it. But eventually, she had to make her way to the couch and sink down. The dogs joined her, lying at her feet and a couple settling on the couch with her.

When Kassandra joined her, she covered her with a light throw. "Comfortable?"

Jayden nodded. "Yes, thanks."

"I'm going to go change out your bed."

Jayden tried to move, but Kassandra eased her down. "I'll be right back." She touched her cheek, so light and delicate Jayden almost wondered if she'd imagined it. With a blink, she was gone, leaving behind her light, lingering scent. Some of the dogs followed her, including Dax, who had become quite taken with her. Jayden smiled and closed her eyes. It felt so good having Kassandra in her home. Sharing a meal with her, sipping wine, just having light conversation as if they were an everyday couple settling in for the evening. It felt good, warm, perfect. Even if they were only friends.

"Where are your sheets?" Kassandra called out.

"In the hall closet." Jayden winced at having to yell. It hurt, and now even breathing seemed to hurt. She decided to rise and join her rather than continue to shout. Slowly, she walked down the hall to the bedroom. She slowed as she came to the doorway. As she reached up for the door frame to steady herself, she caught sight of Kassandra at the bed, Jayden's pillow hugged to her body. She moaned as she briefly inhaled it and then removed the pillowcase.

Fire burned beneath Jayden's cheeks and she knew she should retreat, but the dogs on her heels bounded into the room and onto the bed, startling Kassandra. She turned and dropped the pillow, while the cover remained in her hand. "You scared me," she said, covering her heart with her free hand.

Jayden looked away, unsure what to say. With the wine, she couldn't think quickly enough, and she knew with Kassandra's awkward silence that she knew Jayden had seen her. She tossed the pillowcase on the bed and blushed. "I, um, you really should be resting while I do this."

"I came to help."

"You shouldn't have."

Jayden met her gaze. "But I did."

Kassandra forced a smile and sighed. "Yes, well, I've been wondering what cologne you wear. I really like it."

Jayden's heart pounded in her ears. She wanted to walk to her, cup her face, and kiss her so soft, so deep, she'd crawl into every cell in her body. But Kassandra was embarrassed, and it had been a private moment, not one she'd wanted Jayden to know about. Jayden had to respect that.

"Safari." The word just came out, her voice threatening to cave.

"Oh. I don't think I've ever heard of that one before."

Jayden stood still, not trusting herself to move. "It's men's cologne."

Kassandra continued to pull the sheets from the bed. "You, uh, wear men's cologne?"

"Yes."

"I guess I never even imagined that. Women, you know, wearing men's cologne."

"I like the way it smells. And so do—those I date."

Kassandra tripped over the pile of sheets on the floor but caught herself, straightening with her hand in her hair, obviously flustered. "I'm so clumsy." She laughed, but it sounded nervous. She bent and hugged the sheets and moved toward the door, lower half of her face covered.

Jayden moved to let her by and then walked to the bed to begin putting on the set of clean sheets. Her back spasmed a little, but it honestly felt good to stretch. She struggled with the fitted sheet but finally managed to get it on. When she finished, she lay down, arms out wide, loose sheet over her legs. She exhaled long and slow and fought sleep.

"You look comfortable," Kassandra said, coming up to sit beside her. The blush on her face still remained, and Jayden wondered what she was thinking, feeling.

"I am. It feels good to spread out."

Kassandra wrung her hands. "I could, you know, massage you."

Jayden jerked and closed her eyes in pain. "I don't think that would be a good idea."

Kassandra was silent for a long moment. "Maybe you're right. Maybe some things we shouldn't do as friends." Silence fell between them, and Kassandra sat with her hands in her lap, shoulders relaxed, a sad look on her face. "It's hard for me," she said. "Figuring out this friend thing."

Jayden watched her closely. She wanted to reach up and stroke her jaw, her arm, her hand. "I know what you mean."

"We're okay, though, aren't we? We're good friends, right?"

"You're an amazing friend."

"So are you. You're probably the closest one to me at this point."

"What about your lesbians? They really care about you."

"They do, but they have each other. And besides, it's easy with them because I'm not in lo—" She stopped suddenly.

"What?" Jayden wanted desperately for her to finish her sentence. She wanted to hear her say the words.

Kassandra's phone rang and she plucked it from her pocket and answered. Her face went pale with shock and then distorted in anger.

"Who is this?" She paced. "Who is this? You're not scaring me, you know."

Jayden forced herself to sit up completely. It took her breath away, but she was too focused on Kassandra's conversation. Kassandra yelled into the phone and ended the call. She held the phone in a tight fist as if she wanted to crush it.

"Who was it?" Jayden asked, alarmed.

"I don't know. Just someone heavy breathing."

Jayden carefully slung her legs over the bed. "They didn't say anything?"

"No." She eased herself onto the bed and palmed her forehead. "They never do."

Jayden straightened. "It's happened before?"

Kassandra nodded.

Jayden recalled the fear she'd seen in her after the break-in. How she'd slept with her lights on and bought extra locks. How could she have forgotten?

"What else has happened, Kassandra? And why haven't you told me?"

She shook her head. "My porch light…the lights are gone. Someone unscrewed them, so I put new ones in this morning."

Jayden stood as best as she could. "Come on, we're going to your place."

Kassandra stood alongside her. "Jayden, no. You can't."

"I can and we are."

But Kassandra was insistent. She grabbed Jayden's bicep and squeezed. "No. I took care of it. You need to let me take care of it. And you need to take care of yourself."

"This isn't a nuisance, Kassandra. It's your safety. At least take Dax."

She shook her head again and walked from the room. Jayden followed, though not as quickly. By the time she reached the living room, Kassandra had her purse slung over her shoulder and she had opened the door.

"Kassandra, wait."

She looked back and appeared crestfallen but determined. "I'm sorry, Jayden. I just can't accept help when you're in so much pain. I'll be fine. Just don't worry and I'll handle it." And with that, she closed the door behind her and stepped down the porch steps into the twilight and away from the safety of Jayden and her home.

CHAPTER TWENTY-FIVE

Dawn had yet to break when Kassandra woke. She slipped into her robe and made her way with Lula through the living room to the front door. The days were growing cooler and nights were downright heaven-like, but she'd been too uncomfortable to leave her bedroom window cracked. So she'd slept in the stale, stuffy air of the house, since it was too cool outside for her air to kick on. She unlocked the door and opened it, ready to let some fresh air in. She stepped out for her morning paper and to let Lula relieve herself, but she felt something pierce the sole of her foot instead. She cried out and hopped back. The light filtered out through the door showing her glittering shards of glass on her front porch. She flicked the patio light switch on and off. Nothing. She retreated into the house, leaving a trail of blood along the kitchen floor as she gathered paper towels and a flashlight. She went to wipe her foot, winced, and pulled out a piece of glass. Then she half walked, half hopped back to the front door. She aimed the flashlight at her patio light. The two bulbs were busted and in pieces on the ground. Someone had shattered them, and she'd literally just replaced them.

A chill ran up her spine and gooseflesh erupted along her skin and scalp.

Something moved.

"Kassandra?"

She blinked and placed her hand on the lock of the security door.

"It's me, Brian."

He stood at her thigh-high gate and waved. She wanted to breathe a sigh of relief, but she noticed the chill remained, her hair standing on end.

"Are you okay?" He held up his newspaper. "I was just getting my paper and I swore I heard somebody yelp."

"Yes, yes that was me. I just stepped on a little glass is all."

"Oh, no." He opened the gate and stepped in, looking first at the ground then up at the lights. "Oh, man. Your lights."

A laugh escaped her, a nervous one. "It's no big deal. I was just getting ready to clean it up."

Lula began to bark as he took another step toward her. The light from the flashlight put him in spotlight, and Kassandra thought he looked macabre with a pale distorted face, crooked with a grin. She switched off the flashlight, the image making her uncomfortable. He looked more normal in the dim light.

He pointed to her foot that she was favoring. She could feel the blood trickling off it. She hoped he couldn't see.

"You're hurt."

She looked down as if she didn't know. "Oh, it's fine. Just a little cut."

"A cut? You might have glass embedded in there. Mind if I come in and take a look? I used to be an EMT. I could have you fixed up in no time."

She took in his jeans, nice belt, and tucked in short-sleeved striped polo shirt. He had on sneakers and his hair looked freshly cut. He looked like any average guy. Only...she caught his scent and knew it was cologne. She didn't know what kind it was, but she found it strong and thought it odd that he had it on so early in the morning and on the weekend. She reasoned with herself that maybe he'd just showered and he liked to wear it every day. But a part of her wouldn't accept that, and she hadn't noticed it being so strong before. She moved back and was about to flip the lock to secure the door.

"You know Katelynn and Wendy asked me to kind of keep an eye on you. If they find out I didn't help you in this situation, then...well, you know. I'm a dead man." He smiled.

Katelynn and Wendy came to mind and she relaxed a little. Brian was, after all, their friend. And they'd trusted him enough to set her up with him. She recalled their attempt at a blind date at happy hour and how disastrous it had been. Partly because of her confession.

She lowered her hand. She could use help with her foot since she couldn't see it very well. And she'd definitely need help with the cleanup.

She opened the door. "Come in, please."

He smiled again and stepped carefully along the ground and wiped his shoes on her outside rug. He followed her into the kitchen.

"Looks like you've been bleeding pretty bad."

She sat at the kitchen chair and again pressed paper towels to her foot.

"You have a first aid kit?" He moved behind the counter and opened a cabinet above the sink. He pulled it out. "Oh, good."

She watched him, wondering if that was where he kept his. He seemed to know his way around a kitchen. He placed the plastic box on the counter and dug through it, setting aside what he needed. Then he placed the goods on the table and knelt before her. He took her foot gently. "This might sting a little." He wiped her wound with wet cotton balls, causing her to jerk in surprise and pain. He had soaked them in peroxide and she knew her wound was fizzing. It made her light-headed to think about.

"Hang tight," he said, doing it again with fresh cotton balls. When she clenched the sides of the chair, he soothed her and then blew delicately on her wound. The sensation sent shivers through her, but not the kind of shivers she should enjoy. She shifted, growing uncomfortable, uneasy. His grin didn't help to ease her suddenly pounding heart. He blew again, and this time his hand moved up and down her calf as if he were lightly playing her skin.

"That's it," he said, his voice low and creepy. "Good girl. Just relax."

Kassandra's hair stood up again and she pulled her foot away. "Thanks, I've got it from here."

His boyish eyes flashed and darkened. He stood and tossed the cotton balls on the table. "I didn't get it very clean," he said. "You don't want an infection."

"I know, I'm uh, going to go to my doctor this morning."

"It's Saturday."

She couldn't move; she was frozen to the chair, prey caught in the eyes of the predator. "Brian, I'm fine. I appreciate your help, but I'm going to go back to bed for a while."

"Well, at least let me help you to bed." He was trying to hide the change in attitude and the darkness clouding his eyes.

"No, thank you." She forced herself to stand. "I'm going to call my friend. She'll help me out."

"It's five thirty in the morning," he said.

"I know. We have some things to do today and we want to get an early start." She knew he wasn't buying it. It was a stupid lie, but she wished it were true. Wished Jayden would just know somehow and show. But she was so nervous she couldn't even make it sound convincing.

He took a step toward her, reached out, and touched her arm. "Know what I think? I think there is no friend to call this early. I think you're attracted to me like I am you and you're avoiding being alone with me."

Kassandra swallowed, desperately trying to think. "I...I..." But then she heard crunching and cursing on the patio and a voice.

"Wait, Dax, let me pick you up."

It was Jayden. Kassandra shoved her way past Brian and limped to the door. She opened it quickly, so shocked, so thankful.

"Get in here, now."

Jayden looked alarmed and pale with pain from holding Dax. She stepped inside and set him down. Lula barked and approached him slowly, but Dax wasn't interested. He immediately faced off with Brian and barked, ears back.

"What's going on?" Jayden asked, trying to calm him.

Kassandra grabbed her arm and leaned into her. "Help me," she whispered.

Brian stared at the dog for a moment but then took in Jayden. He did not look like he approved. "This must be the friend," he said. His eyes looked dull, void of humanity. Kassandra couldn't believe the change in him. "Rest assured, I've got it covered, friend. I'm tending to her wound and fixing her light."

Kassandra squeezed Jayden's arm. "No. I said that's not necessary."

"But it is." He clenched his jaw. "You're hurt and the light needs repair."

"I'll take care of it," Jayden said. Kassandra felt her muscles harden as her own sense of warning kicked in.

"You can barely stand," he said, a hint of a grin on his face.

"Who are you, exactly?" Jayden asked.

"I'm Brian, a friend of Kassandra's."

"I've only met him once."

Jayden seemed to sense her fear. "You need to go now."

He smiled wickedly. "Says who?"

"Says me." Kassandra steeled herself.

He moved toward the door, eyes traveling from one to the other. "I guess this is the kind of treatment you get for trying to help someone."

"I guess so, in your case, anyhow," Jayden said, closing the door behind him and bolting the locks.

Kassandra threw herself in her arms. "Thank God you're here! How did you know?"

"I didn't. I was just still concerned from last night, so I came to check things out as soon as I could move well enough. And besides, I wanted to insist you take Dax. I figured you'd be too sleepy to argue. I tried to call."

"Any other morning you would've been right." She thought about her phone. She hadn't checked it that morning yet and it had been in sleep mode. "I didn't hear the phone."

"It made me worry, so I guess it's a good thing. Did he hurt you?" Jayden held her back and searched her eyes.

"No, but he was…creepy. And the way he touched me. Ugh, God."

Jayden walked to the plantation blinds and looked out. "He's still there. Pacing."

Kassandra sat on the couch, hands shaking. Her fight-or-flight mode was still coursing through her body. "If you hadn't come, I don't know what would've happened."

"He frightened you that badly?"

"Yes."

Jayden sat next to her on the couch, and both of the dogs came to them. "Is he a neighbor?"

"Yes. And Katelynn and Wendy set me up with him at happy hour. But I told him I wasn't interested in men anymore."

"Really? I guess that would shock someone. It does me. It also surprised me that your friends know him."

"They do, but I'm beginning to wonder how well."

Jayden glanced back at the door. "It wouldn't surprise me if he's the one who messed with your lights." She stood again and checked the window. "He's still there. I'm calling the cops."

Kassandra hopped to the window. Brian had stopped pacing. He was now just beyond her low patio wall, standing and staring at the front window with his fists at his sides. "Jesus, he looks like something out of a Stephen King novel."

"He looks pissed. Really pissed. Like he's thinking about what to do next." Jayden dialed 911 and spoke to the dispatcher. Kassandra hugged herself at hearing the reality of the situation.

"We're safe in here," Jayden said, turning and leading her back to the couch. She knelt in front of her and eyed her cut.

"The bandages are on the table," Kassandra said.

Jayden crossed to the kitchen and returned with antibacterial ointment and a bandage. She looked at Dax, who stood growling at the window.

"He must still be out there."

"Good, I hope the cops see him." She scratched Lula on the head. Lula seemed to be anxious as well. She was whining and trying to crawl all over her.

Jayden wet a folded paper towel and soaked it in peroxide. She pressed it to the wound. Kassandra was too keyed up to react to the pain.

"It's not very deep," Jayden said. She then applied the ointment with a cotton swab and bandaged the wound. "Do you have thick socks? It will help to protect the bandage."

"My top right drawer," Kassandra said, pointing to her bedroom.

Jayden stood slowly and walked to the bedroom. Kassandra heard her opening and closing the drawer.

"I see you added some curtains to cover your blinds," Jayden said, returning. "They're nice."

"They make me feel safer. Like now no one can see in at all."

Jayden handed over the fleece socks and walked back to the window. She nearly jumped back and snapped the blinds shut. "He's sitting on the wall, staring at the window."

"What?"

Jayden held up a hand to keep her at bay. "Stay there. He might try to do something to the window." Dax barked and growled and Jayden led him away to the couch. They all sat together with Jayden holding Kassandra's hand.

"Thank you for caring enough to come," Kassandra said.

Jayden squeezed her hand. "Of course. You do the same for me."

Dax barked again and they heard shouting. The police were calling out orders. "Come on." Jayden took them to the back bedroom as the shouting grew louder. Kassandra could hear that Brian wasn't cooperating. And after repeated orders, there was more shouting and a scuffle. Her heart raced wildly and Dax went crazy while Lula hid under the bed. Jayden stood guard at the door until the shouting stopped and there was a knock at the door. She crossed the living room, unbolted the door, and opened it a crack. Kassandra came to join her.

"We have the suspect in custody," the officer said. "He resisted, so we are taking him in."

Kassandra opened the door farther. "I think he's the one who damaged my lights."

The officer, who was thick with muscle and sweaty from

the encounter, nodded. "You're safe for now. Someone will take your statement, so please stay put."

Kassandra thanked him and they left the door open for the cooler air. Then she collapsed on the couch as an officer knocked softly and entered, Jayden showing him to a seat. He took her statement, and she reported everything she could recall and more. He made notes and then closed his small notebook and sighed. "As soon as we got his name after the arrest, I called my colleague, Officer Jensen. He's the one who's been investigating your break-in."

"Yes," Kassandra said, growing more and more nervous.

"It seems the surveillance tape from your elderly neighbor, Mr. McRoy, has been cleaned up by our techs. They are going to view it this morning. But it is our belief that our suspect, Brian Edison, may be responsible. Our investigation has been pointing his way."

"What?" Kassandra shook her head. "He's the one who broke into my house?"

"We'll know for sure soon enough. In the meantime, stay by your phone and answer it when we call. Officer Jensen says he's left several messages for you to call him. He's also stopped by."

"I've been at Angel's Wings. I've just been so busy." She didn't tell him that she'd purposely not returned his calls. His messages telling her the man still wasn't caught had only frightened her. Which was another reason why she'd stayed away from home as much as she could.

He stood. "Officer Jensen will be in touch." Jayden showed him out and reassured him that they would remain at the condo, by the phone. She locked the security door and left the main door open. She gave Dax a command and he lay right at the door.

"Come on," Jayden said, holding out her hand. "Let's go lie down."

Kassandra was too drained from stress to argue. She took her hand and stood and they made their way to her bed, where Jayden pulled back the covers and helped her settle in. Then she lay down beside her and spooned her from behind, making her feel so safe and so warm. She closed her eyes, slowed her breathing, and fell asleep.

❖

It was quiet when Kassandra woke, save for the birds and the sound of a distant wind chime. She looked down to see Lula curled next to her stomach and a beautifully tanned hand resting over her arm. Behind her, she heard steady breathing and felt the warm press of a strong body along her back. She snuggled down deeper, wanting to return to sleep. But she glanced at the clock and knew they had to rise, for Officer Jensen would be contacting them at some point.

"Jayden?" she said softly, to which she heard a low mumble. "We need to get up."

"Not yet. Feels so good." Jayden inched closer. Kassandra could feel her breath on the back of her neck.

She burned with a smile and jerked as arousing goose bumps tightened her skin. "I know."

"Can we have a sleepover?" Jayden asked. "I'll bring snacks and scary movies. But you have to promise I can sleep in here, on this wonderful bed, surrounded by goose feathers and lavender."

Kassandra laughed. "Maybe."

"Maybe?"

Jayden popped up behind her, and Kassandra turned to

face her. She found her with a crooked grin, dark messy hair, eyes sparkling in the filtered light coming through the gold curtains. Her cheeks were red with heated sleep.

"Maybe when all this calms down." Kassandra tried not to stare and she tried to sound nonchalant. She didn't want to jump up and down at the idea even though it was what she was doing inwardly.

Jayden seemed to sense her feelings, though, and reached out to touch her face. She stopped herself, hesitated to speak. "Okay, sounds good."

Kassandra closed her eyes, wanting the moment to last. Jayden in her bed, looking beyond gorgeous, feeling so soft, strong, warm next to her. Kassandra knew she'd sleep with her face buried in the pillow Jayden had used.

"We should get up, maybe eat something."

Jayden nodded and cleared the dogs from the bed. She stood and stretched and Kassandra looked away as her T-shirt rose to show a hint of carved abdominal muscles. Jayden was so fit and strong, and each time the realization caught her, it did things to her. Things she didn't quite understand yet, feelings she'd never felt before. Like a dancing butterfly in her stomach, or a ball of fire in her throat. One second she felt so heavy with heat she thought she'd combust, and the next second she felt so light she could float away.

She remade the bed and Jayden helped her and then stepped closer to help her walk to the living room.

"How's the foot?"

"A little better." The wound felt tight, like it would tear open again, but she didn't let on. Just walked as carefully as she could.

"Thirsty?" Jayden called from the kitchen. "How about some iced tea?"

Kassandra stiffened as she recalled Brian knowing exactly where her first aid kit was.

"Oh. God." Bile rose in her throat. She sank onto the couch.

"What was that?"

"Yes, tea is fine." How could she have been so stupid? Could it have been any more obvious?

Dax ran to the door and barked seconds before Kassandra heard the squeak of her gate. Jayden entered carrying two glasses. She set them down on the coffee table as the doorbell rang. She motioned for Kassandra to stay on the couch.

"Good boy, Dax." She glanced out the blinds. "It's a man. Looks like a cop."

She unlocked the door and opened it.

"Hi, I'm Officer Jensen. Can I speak with Ms. Haden, please?"

Jayden welcomed him and opened the door, telling Dax to be good. Officer Jensen entered, and he looked the same as he had the last time she'd seen him, only now he was wearing street clothes.

"Ms. Haden." He nodded and shook her hand as she rose the best she could.

"Officer Jensen, please, have a seat." She offered him the ivory chair across from the couch. "This is my friend Jayden Beaumont."

He shook Jayden's hand before he settled in on the chair. "Is it okay if I speak freely in front of your friend?"

"Sure." She grew nervous with what he had to say. His demeanor was very serious.

"I would've called, but the information we gathered today…I think I needed to tell you in person."

"What is it?" Her heart tripled in pace.

Jayden settled down next to her.

"It seems as though Brian Edison, the man who caused a disturbance this morning, is your burglar. We found several photos of you on his person this morning, and based on his behavior and some statements he made, we got a warrant to search his home."

Kassandra swallowed with difficulty. "And you found my things."

He cleared his throat. "Yes, ma'am." He opened his satchel and retrieved a file. He removed a photo and showed her. It was a photo of panties, five altogether, all of them hers. She clenched her jaw and looked away. She felt so exposed and sick to her stomach she could hardly breathe.

"They're yours?" he asked.

"Yes."

He tucked the photo back in the folder and removed more. Kassandra nodded at the photos of her jewelry and other personal keepsakes.

Officer Jensen returned the photos and placed the satchel on the floor. He clasped his hands. "We also found more photos of you in his home. Seventy-three altogether."

Kassandra closed her eyes, feeling dizzy. A warm hand covered hers and squeezed.

"He's been stalking you for some time."

Kassandra took a deep breath and exhaled. "What now?"

"We press charges. Fortunately, we have complaints from two other women as well. One at his workplace and another who works at the corner store. Neither knew enough about him to report him. But today's events tied it all together. We found their photos as well as written notes about where they worked. The same information he had on you."

"Has he ever hurt anyone?" Jayden asked.

"No previous record," he said. "But it was obvious he's

been escalating from Peeping Tom type of behavior to stealing undergarments to breaking and entering. If he hadn't been caught, the next step could've been very, very bad." He stood. "We'll keep in contact. For now, try and relax. He can't seem to make bail. I'll have someone call you with instructions on how to get a restraining order. That will keep him away from here."

Kassandra hugged herself. She felt like Brian Edison had touched her everywhere. She wanted to scrub her skin and every inch of her home. She just wanted everyone out so she could lock herself in and the world out.

Officer Jensen left with Jayden showing him out. Kassandra sat motionless. Jayden came to her, tried to talk to her, but Kassandra was gone, scrubbing her mind before she started in on everything else. She saw Jayden's face, her concerned eyes. But how could she explain how she felt? How could she explain it to anyone?

"I think I need to be alone," she said softly.

Jayden reared back a little and blinked. "Okay." She stood from her kneel. "I won't argue with you, but you have to keep Dax."

Kassandra nodded, staring beyond her.

Jayden touched her face. "Don't check out on me, Kassandra. Please don't do that. Because I'm never going to check out on you."

Kassandra met her eyes briefly. "I can't make any promises," she said.

Jayden bent, kissed her forehead, slipped into her shoes, and walked out the door.

Kassandra limped to the door, bolted the locks, and headed straight for the shower. She was going to scrub herself raw and hope against hope that she could wash Brian Edison away.

CHAPTER TWENTY-SIX

Jayden entered the office and checked her phone for texts. It had been two weeks since the Brian incident, and Jayden had been keeping close tabs on Kassandra, who texted her a few times a day on her days away from the kennel. Today, however, she was due to come in and Jayden was excited, for she had quite the surprise for her.

She stopped at Allie's desk, grabbed a few messages, and walked to her desk where a young man sat. She tossed the messages on the desk and sat in her chair. She smiled.

"Tony, as always, good to see you."

The young man returned the smile. "Is she here?"

"Not yet."

"Man, I can't wait to see her. It's been a long time."

"I know. She'll be thrilled."

"I hope so."

"She will."

He squirmed in his chair and fiddled with his ball cap, which was in his lap. For a boy without much parental supervision, he seemed to have very good manners. It had taken some time and lots of finagling with her friends, but Jayden had finally found him newly placed in a foster home. He'd started a new school, and so far, had been in much less trouble. It helped that his foster parents were good, patient people. They'd fostered one of her former kids a few years back and she knew them to be good people. They'd told her Tony was still pretty quiet but that he seemed happier on days when he worked at the kennel.

"No one has told her, right?" he asked.

Jayden shook her head. "Nope."

His knee bounced. "I really appreciate you finding me and offering me this job."

"You had a good reference," Jayden said, referring to Kassandra. "If Ms. Haden likes you, then that says a lot to me. The second test…the dogs. And so far, they approve."

"Is there a third test?"

"Mm-hmm. The fam. The Angel's Wings family."

"How do I pass that?"

"Just be yourself, work hard, be good to the dogs, nice to people. You'll do fine."

He wiped nervous-looking hands on his long denim shorts. His knee continued to bounce.

"She's here!" Allie called out as Jayden stood and saw Kassandra's car pulling in. The group in the office gathered around Tony, and Jayden crossed to meet Kassandra at the counter. She entered slowly, just as she did on any other day, head down, purse on her shoulder, eyes covered by sunglasses. When she finally looked up at the counter, she jerked a little at Jayden's presence. She smiled.

"What are you doing?" she asked with a laugh.

Jayden shrugged. "Just wanted to greet my friend at the door."

"Oh-kay," Kassandra said, walking beyond the waist-high door, which Jayden held for her. "Why?"

"Just to be polite. You know, 'Hi, honey, how was your day?' kind of thing." She tried not to break out in a grin. She walked by her side as Kassandra continued to look at her curiously.

"Seriously, what is up?" They stopped in the middle of the room and Kassandra eyed the group of workers, gathered in a group, all grins.

Again, Jayden shrugged. "I don't know. Maybe we have something of a surprise for you."

"A surprise?"

Jayden nodded at the group and they all moved outward, showing Tony standing in the middle.

Kassandra looked at him for a second with complete disbelief. Then she blinked and let out a scream. "Oh my God!" She rushed at him and enveloped him in her arms. He laughed and hugged her back and they spun like giddy children. "What in the world? Are you really here?" She grabbed his face.

"It's me," he said. "I'm really here."

"But when? How?" She looked back to Jayden, who was smiling so hard it hurt.

"Ms. Beaumont, she hunted me down. She knows my new fosters."

"She does, huh?" Kassandra placed a hand on her hip. "Guess I have to hug you, too." She looked at the group as a whole. "Guess I owe everybody a hug."

Jayden laughed as she hugged one person after another. When she got to Jayden, she hesitated but then embraced her quickly. "Thank you," she whispered. "Thank you so much."

Jayden released her as she pulled away, seemingly overcome with emotion. "How did you do this without me knowing?"

"We met on your days off," Tony said. "But this day," he said. "This day is the best by far."

Kassandra tugged on his baseball cap. "I'd say so."

"Today is also special for a couple of other reasons,"

Jayden said, quieting the group. "Kassandra, I—we'd like to offer you a permanent position here at the kennel. When your semester ends, of course. We are willing to work around your school schedule if you want to return to get your degree in counseling."

A look of complete disbelief washed over Kassandra's face. Her mouth fell open and she stared at Jayden as if she wasn't sure what she'd just heard.

"You can go back to school, Kassandra. Do what you really want to do."

"Yeah, and work here," Gus said. "Because we aren't letting you leave again."

The teens all voiced their agreement and Tony swatted her on the arm. "Say something, Ms. H. Don't leave us hanging."

"I'm just so surprised. Pleasantly surprised."

"Is that a yes?" Billy asked.

"Yes. Yes, of course it is. I'd be honored to be included in this group."

The teens cheered and collapsed into her, hugging her. Jayden smiled and noticed that Kassandra's eyes never left hers. She looked truly happy, truly grateful. And nothing had ever lit Jayden up from the inside like seeing Kassandra so happy. She grinned, felt tears threaten, and clapped her hands for attention, needing to change topics before she cried in front of her staff.

"There's one more surprise today and a reason to celebrate." She looked to the warehouse door and nodded. Gus entered with Cooper on a leash. He handed him over and knelt and said good-bye. When he stood, he wiped tears from his eyes.

"Cooper is going to his forever home today," Jayden said. She eyed the clock. "Any minute now." The group cheered, but then the noise lowered to mumbles as they all said good-bye to him, one by one. Kassandra also knelt and told him good-bye. She, too, teared up.

Jayden followed, rubbing his soft furry chest. He placed a paw on her shoulder. "I'm going to miss you, buddy. So very much. But John will love you and pay you so much more attention than I ever could. I love you." She kissed his head and nuzzled his neck, inhaling his scent. Gus had just bathed him for his trip home and he smelled fresh and clean, ready for his new life. Moments like these were what the kennel was all about. But they were always bittersweet.

The bell on the door jingled as John rushed in. Allie let him in through the counter door and he bolted for Jayden, sliding on his knees in front of Cooper, who wagged his tail. "I'm here, I'm here." He hugged Cooper. "I'm not late, boy. I'd never be late to get you."

Jayden again held back tears. She could hardly look at the boy, much less hear his love for the dog. It burned deep in her chest, and she almost needed to excuse herself to go break down into tears. Cooper and John had their time together, but their time also paralleled her time with Kassandra. And as she caught her eye, she saw that she too was tearing up and not just because of a boy and his dog.

It was a quiet, heavy moment. One of deep emotion. Kassandra touched her chest, right at her heart. Jayden did the same, not knowing if Kassandra meant anything by it. When she smiled, Jayden figured she did.

"The big day is here," John's mother said, joining the small crowd.

"And to think, you actually doubted it would ever come," Jayden teased her, having to tear her eyes away from Kassandra.

"I know, can you believe it? I should've known my son better."

"Can we go now, Mom?" John looked at Jayden. "We're taking him to the pet store. Going to buy him everything he needs."

"That's great." She shook his hand as he stood and handed him the leash. Jayden walked them to the counter. "He's been microchipped as you requested, and all his pertinent papers are in here." She retrieved Cooper's good-bye bag and handed it over. "The vet information is in there for his free visit. But you need to do that within thirty days. And as always, if you have any questions or concerns, let me know. I do suggest you get him a pillow bed rather than a crate. He doesn't like being locked up. And he's very much house trained, so you could get a pet door. Overall, he's a wonderful dog and I think you all will be very, very happy."

"He's gonna sleep with me," John said. "But we will still get him his very own bed."

"Thank you so much, Jayden." John's mother reached out and shook her hand.

"My pleasure."

"Come on, boy! Time to go get some toys." John and Cooper ran through the counter door and pushed out the main door. His mother waved and disappeared behind them. Jayden stood and watched them go.

"You did a very good thing there," Kassandra said, placing a hand on her shoulder.

"Mmm."

"Can I talk to you for a second?"

Jayden felt her lower her hand and press up against her. Her breathing grew short and quick as they stood like that, skin on skin, body pressed to body, Kassandra slightly behind her. She reached down and covered Jayden's hand with her own. Jayden inhaled sharply.

"Please, I really need to talk to you," Kassandra whispered.

Jayden turned her head slightly, wanting to feel her breath. "Where do you want to go?"

"Your place." She squeezed her hand.

"Okay."

They crossed the room, Kassandra walking behind her at a distance. The group was chatting with excitement and no one seemed to notice as they slipped out the door. Jayden turned to her as she walked across the lot toward her house. Kassandra moved slowly, grinning slightly. Jayden swallowed against a rising lump in her throat as she considered what was happening. She knew she shouldn't get too excited, but there seemed to be little doubt in Kassandra's intent. She had the look of hunger, moving with seduction, never tearing her eyes away from Jayden.

When they reached the door, Jayden waited for her. When she felt the press of her body up against hers, she let out a shaky breath.

"Are you sure?" Jayden asked, hand trembling as she reached for the doorknob.

"Yes."

Jayden closed her eyes. She couldn't believe it was finally happening. Her normally confident attitude in such matters was missing, nowhere to be found. She was excited, aroused, and surprisingly…nervous.

"Open the door, Jayden," Kassandra said.

Jayden managed to turn the knob and push open the door. The dogs greeted them with excitement, some of them bolting in through the dog door. Kassandra shooed them, gave them a calm command, and told them all to lie down. She heard the door close behind her and then something else. The bolt of the lock engage.

She shivered with growing desire.

"Look at me, Jayden."

Jayden turned. Kassandra walked toward her and reached out to touch her face. "Look at me like you did the first time we met. Like you want me so badly it hurts."

Jayden inhaled sharply, took her all in, and trembled from head to toe.

"Yes, like that." She inched closer, cupping her jaw with her right hand. "Now, tell me again what you want. Tell me that you want to read the book of my life. From page one to infinity."

Jayden saw the desire in her eyes, heard it in her lowered voice. She stepped into her, nearly touched her lips to hers, but instead lightly kissed her cheek and whispered in her ear. "I want to read the book of your life, from page one to infinity."

Kassandra shook and exhaled. "Oh God, Jayden. I want you so bad. I can't fight it anymore. I think about you day and night. I can't sleep. I can't focus. I hear your voice and it floors me. I see your face and it wrecks me. I inhale your scent and my legs melt. And when I'm close to you, like now, touching you, no matter how delicate our connection, I feel it between my legs. This tingling, pulsing, swelling. Like all my blood has left my body to rush there. And I can't think of anything else but how I want you to touch me there. With your fingers...with your mouth. Oh, God, I can't take it anymore."

Jayden moaned as her own center flooded with desire. She tugged Kassandra closer, stared wildly, deeply into her eyes, and then crushed her with a hot, hungry kiss. The feel of her mouth against hers, so hot, wet, eager, she moaned again and then nearly collapsed when she felt Kassandra press back with her own tongue. Jayden lifted her then, hands firmly under her thighs. Kassandra cried out with surprise but then continued to kiss her. So madly, so intensely, Jayden had trouble steering them across the living room, down the hallway, and to the bedroom. Once there, she tore her mouth away from her and set her on the bed.

"The dogs," Kassandra said, tugging on Jayden's polo shirt, like she didn't want her to walk away from her.

"The dogs," Jayden said, shooing them out. She pulled away from Kassandra only long enough to close the door, then she crossed back to her, bent, and kissed her long and heavy. Kassandra tugged her closer by the hips, then ran her hands up under her shirt.

"Take it off," she said, looking up at her.

Jayden stripped off her shirt and threw it down, chest heaving. She tried to bend to kiss her again, but Kassandra stopped her. "Your bra," she said. "Off."

Jayden straightened and looked down at her.

"Please, I want to see you."

Jayden reached behind, unclasped her bra, slid it off, and tossed it aside. Her small, taut breasts puckered as she breathed, as if they anticipated Kassandra touching them.

"I—you're so strong. So beautiful. Can I touch you?" She reached up and Jayden took her hand and kissed it and then placed it on her abdomen. Kassandra's breath shook as she lightly ran her fingers over her stomach and then up to her breasts where she teased her nipples with the delicate strokes of the backs of her fingers. Jayden shuddered, trying so hard to control herself and stand still.

"Does it feel good?"

"Yes."

"I want to make you feel good," she said. "It's all I want to do. I think I could…climax just pleasing you."

Jayden closed her eyes, knowing the feeling all too well.

"Can I take off your shorts?" Kassandra asked.

Jayden nodded. Kassandra trailed her hands down to her hips and unbuttoned her khaki cargo shorts. Then she slid them down below her thighs to her ankles and Jayden stepped out of them and kicked them aside, along with her shoes. Kassandra looked up at her, fingers teasing around the waistband of her boy shorts.

"May I?"

"Are you sure?" Jayden asked again.

Kassandra didn't blink, didn't hesitate. "Yes."

Jayden tried to breathe steadily and nodded. She closed her eyes as Kassandra gently and carefully lowered her shorts to her ankles. Jayden jerked as she felt the delicate kiss of her breath as she lowered herself and then came back up again to breathe on her center.

"You're wet," Kassandra said. "I can see it."

"Mmm." She felt dizzy, crazy. Like if she wasn't touched soon she'd faint from desire alone.

"I want to touch you," Kassandra said. Jayden jerked again as she felt the light press of a fingertip on her labia. "Here."

Jayden clenched her jaw.

"Can I?"

"Yes."

"Do you want me to? Do you want me to touch you there?"

Jayden shook and clenched her hands into fists. "God, yes."

"Open your eyes," Kassandra said. "I want to look into your eyes as I touch you there."

Jayden opened her eyes. Kassandra held her gaze as she traced her fingers down Jayden's smooth labia and into her folds.

Jayden's knees went weak as she found her.

"Oh fuck," Kassandra whispered. "You're so hot and

slick." She moved from the pool of slick desire up to her clit, where she stroked.

Jayden's hips jerked involuntarily and she bit into her lower lip.

"Dear God, you feel so good. So slick and soft."

"Kassandra," she said with great difficulty.

"Yes?" Her beautiful eyes were lidded with seduction. She was truly enjoying herself.

"I can't take much more."

She grinned. "Good."

"I want to feel you," Jayden said. "While you feel me."

Kassandra stared up into her. "No, I don't want to stop."

Jayden groaned and her eyes rolled back in her head. Her hips went insane as Kassandra sped up her stroking. "Am I doing it, right? Am I touching you the way you like? Because this is what I like when I touch myself."

Jayden gripped her shoulders. "Yes. Kassandra, yes." The thought of her touching herself sent her over and she thrust wildly into her hand and came hard and long. She cried out and clenched her eyes, jerking and thrusting.

"Oh God, Jayden. You're coming. You're coming in my hand. Oh, God, it's so beautiful. The way you feel in my hand, the way you're moving, beautiful muscles flexing and straining. Come into me, come into my hand."

Jayden threw her head back and cried out again. She lost all control then and fucked her hand as hard and as fast as she could, desperate for every last bit of pleasure her fingers were offering, until eventually she stilled and her legs shook and Kassandra milked her a little more, causing her to jerk a few more times.

Jayden fell to her knees, completely spent, breath heaving. She rested her head in Kassandra's lap and went limp.

Kassandra stroked her hair, traced her jaw with her fingertip. "I can't wait to put my mouth on you," she said.

Jayden struggled to speak. "I can't even imagine that at this point."

Kassandra rubbed her back, teased her with the slight press of her short nails. Jayden could feel her own slickness as Kassandra rubbed up and down her back.

"I loved it," Kassandra said. "I can't believe how much I loved it. Touching you like that. Making you come."

Jayden lifted her head. "I could tell." No one had ever brought her to her knees before. No one had ever touched her like that, played her flesh like that. It was usually all about them, about her taking control and doing them. She didn't know why things were different this time, but she honestly didn't care. It had been incredible, the best, most body-wracking orgasm she'd ever had. And now she was lying in Kassandra's lap, in pure heaven.

Beyond the bedroom door the dogs barked, and Jayden swore she could hear the doorbell.

"Shit," she said as she sat back and stood. She pulled on her clothes.

"Should I hide?" Kassandra asked, handing her her shirt.

"No. No way."

"I'm not sure how the teens will take this."

Jayden laughed. "You think they don't know how we feel about each other?"

Kassandra's eyes widened. "They do?"

Jayden stepped into her shoes. "They knew before we did."

Jayden opened the bedroom door and soothed the barking dogs. Kassandra followed her and stood behind her as she opened the front door. A woman Jayden had never seen before stood smiling coyly at her. She had on a short white dress.

"Jayden," she said. "They said I could just come find you."

Jayden shook her head in confusion. "Okay. Who are you exactly?"

She looked Jayden up and down and licked her red lips. "I'm your dream come true."

Jayden felt Kassandra tense behind her.

"Don't be shy. I know you've been expecting me. And believe me, baby, the wait will have been worth it."

Jayden felt bile rise in her throat as panic came over her. What was happening? And why now? She turned to try to explain to Kassandra, but she was already hurt and angry and shoving her way out the door.

Jayden chased after her. "Kassandra, wait. Please. Just stop."

Kassandra waved her off, storming off. "Leave me alone, Jayden. Go see to your women. And to think I bought into your act, thinking you really cared about me."

"I do!"

Kassandra turned. "Bullshit! It was all just a game to get me, wasn't it? Well, you got me. Feel good about yourself now?" She turned and stormed into the office.

Jayden stood staring. She'd just had everything and lost everything in an instant. How was that even possible?

CHAPTER TWENTY-SEVEN

K assandra poured herself more wine and took a hearty sip. Next to her, the outdoor fireplace warmed her left side, trying to lure her into some sort of peace. But peace, she knew from the last week's experience, wasn't easy in coming.

"We're going to have to call an Uber for you if you keep on," Wendy said, teasing her. She tipped her wineglass to her and took her own hearty sip. Happy hour was in full effect and nearing its end as the sun lowered in the sky, painting the clouds pink and purple just beyond the patio. Katelynn offered Kassandra some nachos, but Kassandra politely declined. She'd suddenly become very picky about her food lately. Nothing sounded appealing. And nothing seemed to get to her, touch her insides. Not even the beautiful sunset in front of her. She felt dead. Dead inside. And she knew why.

Her friends knew too, and they'd done a good job of avoiding the topic so far. A world record for them at ten minutes in.

"I can't tell you again how sorry I am over Brian," Katelynn said. She shook her head. "I just had no idea."

"You couldn't have known," Kassandra said. "The cops said he probably followed me to your house one day and then made it a point to befriend you."

"God, that's beyond scary," Wendy said. "What a freaking psycho."

Kassandra stared off after the painted sky.

"We just thank God you're okay," Katelynn said. "And like it or not, we do feel responsible."

"Don't." She sipped more wine. "I'm fine. He hasn't been around. He can't make bail, and the cops are mounting evidence against him. I'm not worried about it."

She wasn't really worried about anything anymore. She just did what needed to be done with little thought or emotion. And truth be told, it had really helped her at work. She'd told the teacher to get her own damn coffee just that morning. And soon after that she'd told the secretary it wasn't her job to clean up after staff meetings. It was hers. That had led to a nasty letter from the principal, who led the staff in snobbiness, to send her a letter about being a team player. She hadn't even read the whole thing, just deleted it and did her job. To top it off, when she'd left that evening, the office staff didn't bid her a good evening, which had caused her to laugh as she'd walked to her car.

She'd driven to happy hour with the windows down, relishing the thought of buying out her contract and starting school as soon as she could. Tony was no longer at the school; most days she was bored sitting in the library alone. She'd miss reading to the kids, but she could volunteer and do that. No, she knew now she was needed elsewhere. And come Christmas break, she was putting in her notice and starting school in January for counseling. She couldn't wait.

"I'm quitting my job," she said, knowing it would set her friends off. "I'm going back to school in January to get my master's in counseling. I've already applied and been accepted and spoken to an advisor." She drank more wine as Katelynn and Wendy sat stunned. "It's what I really want, and I'm a little nervous about such a big change, so I could really use the support."

Katelynn grabbed her hand. "Of course you have our support. We just want you to be happy, remember?"

"We all know the job—or should I say the people at the job—suck. I don't blame you for wanting something different."

There was more silence and Wendy dug into the nachos. Katelynn stared at her with contentment, but her eyes gave away some concern. Kassandra knew what was coming next.

"Just ask," Kassandra said. "I know you're dying to."

Katelynn looked to Wendy and Wendy spoke. "What exactly happened with Jayden?"

Kassandra thought she could handle hearing her name, but she had to grip the table in order to control the powerful feelings it stirred. "I just don't think she's ready for a serious relationship." The words stung, as did the memory of the attractive woman standing at Jayden's door, beckoning her. It almost made her physically sick. To think Jayden had been expecting her all along and she'd still gone ahead and made love with Kassandra. How could she have missed it? Was Jayden just like Brian? Some sort of chameleon? Or was it her? Was she just unable to read people somehow?

"Another woman?" Wendy asked.

Kassandra swallowed more wine, but it was painful. "Yes."

"Really?" Katelynn said. "I just didn't get that vibe from her. Not the way you talk about her."

"I think I'm just clueless when it comes to reading people."

"Don't think like that," Wendy said. "Some people enjoy misleading and manipulating. That's not on you."

"I just..." Kassandra said. "I just didn't think it of her either. Not after what...we did."

Katelynn leaned forward. "You mean you..."

Kassandra looked away. "We did something, yes. And it was incredible. I can't get it out of my head, that's how good it was. Like it was some kind of drug I tried for the first time. I just want more and more, and that's what makes it hurt all the more. I had her, felt her, was one with her, and then *wham*, it was all slammed in my face when that woman arrived."

"What woman?" Wendy asked.

Kassandra shrugged. "A really hot one. And she said Jayden had been expecting her and that she wanted to, you know, rock her world, so to speak."

"Oh, Jesus," Katelynn said. "What did Jayden say?"

"She acted like she didn't know her and then she tried to chase after me. But I wouldn't hear her out. I was too vulnerable, too torn up inside."

"That's rough, Kassie," Wendy said. "I'm so sorry."

Katelynn poured them more wine and passed the glass to Kassandra. "Oh, honey."

"Well, in Jayden's defense, you did make her promise you'd just be friends."

"You're not helping, honey."

"No, seriously. Maybe she did date. Would that be wrong? As far as she knew, Kassandra didn't want her."

Kassandra drank her wine, fighting back tears. "You don't understand. You don't understand how she was with me. It was like I was the only person in the world." She downed her glass and stood a little unsteadily. Katelynn rose with her.

"You need to come home with us."

"No, I want to be alone. You know I heal better that way."

"Let us call you a cab. You can't drive like this."

"No. I got it."

Katelynn gave Wendy a look and she too stood. She

leafed out some cash and tossed it on the table. They helped Kassandra out to the car.

"What am I gonna do?" Kassandra said, climbing in and leaning over. "I'm so lost in her."

Wendy drove and Katelynn tried to soother her. "If she's meant to be, it will work out. If not, you just heal and move on."

"Oh God. She has another woman. How can it work out?"

"Sometimes things aren't what they seem," Wendy said. "Remember that. And when it comes to relationships with women…you have to remember some can be very aggressive. If they want someone, they don't take no for an answer, whether she has someone else or not."

"What?" Kassandra's mind spun.

"Just relax and try to push it all from your mind for the time being," Katelynn said. "Wendy can give you advice some other time."

"I'm trying to tell her it might not be Jayden's fault. Remember when we first started how aggressive your ex was? It took several weeks for her to stop showing up, declaring her love for you. It didn't matter that you told her no. It didn't matter that you had me. Remember?"

Katelynn sighed. "Yes, unfortunately. But Kassandra doesn't need to think about it at all right now. She just needs to go home and relax."

Kassandra considered Wendy's words, focused on them when she could, and then drifted off when she couldn't grasp rational thought. Soon, the darkness took her for good, and when she awoke again, she was being helped down her sidewalk and placed on her couch, dogs licking her face. Katelynn removed her shoes and left her on her side. She placed her cell phone in her hand.

"Call if you need anything." She kissed her cheek. "Good night, Kassie."

They left her alone, locking the door after them. Within a few minutes, she fell asleep with tears running down her face and the memory of that attractive woman standing at Jayden's door.

CHAPTER TWENTY-EIGHT

Jayden tried Kassandra's phone one last time as she pulled into her parking lot and killed the engine to her truck. The phone went straight to voice mail. Jayden had considered leaving her a message, but she needed to say the things she had to say in person. It had been a little over a week since she'd left her house crying, and Jayden had been ripped to pieces over the whole thing. She'd been going over and over it in her mind. Should she have chased after her? Called her numerous times every day pleading her case? She knew Kassandra better than that. She was worth more than that. She deserved to hear things in person.

The condo complex was silent as she walked up the sidewalk. Some doors were open for the cool weather, and she could see the flashes of televisions through the security screen doors. One man was grilling and she could smell the tangy barbecue. Her stomach protested at the lack of food lately, but she swallowed against it, refusing to give in. How could she eat when Kassandra was suffering, thinking the worst of her? Jayden couldn't even fully imagine what was going through her head. Especially after what they'd shared in her bedroom. The pain, the betrayal, it must be devastating.

She came to her gate, opened it, and stood at her door.

The porch light she'd repaired came on, and Dax immediately started barking. She couldn't help but smile and she was glad he was still there. She hoped Kassandra still wanted him. With a deep breath, she pressed the doorbell. It was seven o'clock on a Friday night. She hoped she was home.

Both dogs barked and Jayden heard movement near the door. She called out. "It's me, it's Jayden."

There was a pause in movement. A quick flick of the blinds. A bolt disengaged. Then the other. The door pulled open and Kassandra peeked out. Jayden inhaled at the sight of her sunken eyes and pale skin. She looked like she hadn't eaten or slept in days.

"Kassandra, are you okay?" It was the first thing out of her mouth.

Kassandra stared through her. "I'm fine."

Dax hopped into the air behind her, excited. "Dax, calm."

Kassandra blinked and seemed to focus. "Oh, I'm sorry." She unlocked the security door and opened it. "Please, come in."

Jayden entered, eyes still trained on her. "Thank you."

Kassandra crossed to the closet and retrieved a leash. "He's been a great dog. Really helped me to feel safe these past few weeks. I don't know what I would've done without him."

She handed it over. Jayden closed her hand over hers instead. "I didn't come for Dax."

Kassandra met her gaze for the first time. Pain blew across her eyes like clouds moving in on a storm. "Oh, well, I'm not going anywhere."

"Please, Kassandra, can we just talk?"

"About what?"

"About what happened. I need to explain."

Kassandra walked to her bedroom and collapsed on

her bed. She hugged a pillow and stared into space. Jayden followed and noted that her eyes looked glossed over as if fresh from tears. It tore at her heart.

"Honestly, Jayden, I don't think I can bear to hear it. I just don't think I can."

Jayden sat, desperate to talk, to get her to hear. "That woman at the kennel, I didn't know her. It was the one Mel sent a long time ago, the one that never showed. She's who I thought you were that first day."

"You expect me to believe that?" She rolled over and faced her window. Lula jumped up and snuggled with her while Dax snuggled up against her back. Jayden wanted so badly to crawl into bed with them and hold her.

"I had hoped you would. But no, I didn't expect you to. Which is why—"

The doorbell rang and Dax took off in an insane bark. Jayden rose. "I think I know who that is." She crossed back to the door and opened it.

"Am I at the right place?" Mel asked, hand on hip.

"Yes, now get in here and be sincere."

Mel entered and followed her to the bedroom.

"Kassandra, Mel has something she wants to say to you."

Kassandra didn't bother to turn, she just squeezed her pillow tighter.

Mel cleared her throat. "Kassandra, I owe you an apology. I never gave you a real shot because I thought you would only hurt Jayden. It was my fault the woman showed up. I'm the one that asked her to come to the kennel to seduce Jayden. She just did it a few weeks too late. Anyway, I was supposed to find her and stop it and I didn't and I've been kind of a bitch to you. I'm sorry. I just really love Jayden, you know, and I want her to be happy. Now I can see that it's you that makes her happy. So please, don't think she was messing around on you or even thinking about it. Because trust me, even though you were both insisting you were just friends, this girl's only thoughts and actions were about you. She even said she'd love you if you moved on with someone else. That as long as she could be in your life somehow, it would make her happy."

Kassandra wiped a tear, and Jayden began shoving Mel out the door to the living room.

"What? Jesus."

"You didn't have to say all that." Jayden ran a hand through her hair.

"Why not? You said to tell the truth."

"Nothing, just, thank you, you can go now."

Mel shook her head. "Fine, I'll go. You're welcome." She let herself out the security door and Jayden closed the big door and locked it behind her. She returned to the bedroom slowly. Kassandra was sitting on the edge of the bed, head in her hands.

She didn't look up. "So you wanted me even though you promised to be friends?"

Jayden bit her lip. She closed her eyes. "Yes."

"Why?"

"Because I couldn't help myself."

"But you never would've made a move on me."

"Never."

"Because of your promise."

"Yes."

Kassandra looked up at her. She stood, tears marking her face. She fingered her hair and tucked it behind her ears. Jayden couldn't help but smile at the sight.

"What?" Kassandra asked.

"That thing. I like it when you," she motioned with her hand, "do that thing where you tuck your hair behind your ears. It lets me know you're nervous."

"Does it?"

"Yes."

"Know what you do? You bite your lip."

Jayden relaxed her mouth. "Yeah, I guess I do."

Kassandra stepped closer. "So what now, Beaumont? You got any more women I need to know about?"

"No."

"Swear?"

"Swear."

"I'm a bit buzzed, you know. A little too much wine this evening."

Jayden felt her face fall with disappointment. She wanted her to remember the things she'd said. "Should I go, then?"

"God no." She stepped closer. Reached out, touched her arm. Jayden inhaled sharply. "I want you to stay and take full advantage of me."

Jayden shuddered. "I don't think—"

"I don't want you to think. I don't want you to do what you think is right. I want you to do what it is you want. What we both want. I want you to take me, Jayden." She stepped into her, reached up and ran her finger down Jayden's lips. "Now."

Jayden could hardly hear the last whispered word, her heart was pounding so hard in her ears. She knew she should tuck her in bed and fall asleep with her, make love in the morning if she still wanted to. But Kassandra was draining all reason from her body with her touch. As if she were some sort of magical being who could do such things with a touch of a finger. She stood on her toes and lightly kissed her lips. Snuck out her tongue and toyed with her desire.

Jayden groaned and took her in her arms and took possession with her mouth. She dove deep into her with her tongue and lifted her so that her legs were straddling her. She walked her to the bed and collapsed with her, crawling atop her, like a hungry wolf over prey. "I want you," she said. "I want you so bad, Kassandra." She kissed her again and ran her hands up her blouse, tracing the tracks with her mouth. Kassandra made noises of pleasure as she writhed beneath her, scraping her short nails along her back. Jayden stopped, sat up, and tore off her T-shirt.

"Yes," she said into Kassandra's ear. "Dig your nails into me. Make me yours."

"I will," Kassandra said. "Oh God, I will." And she moaned and drug her nails down her back once again as Jayden found her neck and devoured it. "You're mine," she said. "Jayden, you're mine."

"Mmm, yes, I am." Jayden bit her delicate flesh and rose again to remove her bra.

"I want to taste them," Kassandra said.

"Not yet." Jayden pinned her and then went to work on the buttons of her blouse.

"Tear it," Kassandra breathed.

Jayden laughed and tore it open. Kassandra sat up, ripped it off her arms, and then tore off her bra to expose her full, perky breasts. Jayden shoved her back down, held down her arms, and took her nipples in her mouth, sucking and lightly nibbling. Kassandra writhed and shook her head from side to side. She called Jayden's name and begged for release.

"Oh God, if you don't stop I'm going to come. I'm going to come, Jayden." Jayden stopped, grinned, and blew on her. Kassandra twitched and sucked in air between her teeth. "Jayden, Jesus. It's going straight between my legs."

"Is it?" Jayden teased her.

"Yes."

"Down here." Jayden released her and allowed her own hand to drift slowly downward to her center. She pressed her lightly and Kassandra bucked her hips. "Right here? Is this the spot?" She stroked her up and down, feeling the mound of heat beneath her fingers.

Kassandra was lost for breath, squeezing her arm. "Yes. You know it is."

"Do I?"

"Yes, don't, don't tease me."

"I won't tease you, love. I'll give it all to you. That's what you want, right?"

Kassandra struggled for breath. "Yes."

"You want me to give it to you until you can't take it anymore."

"Yes." She bucked. "God, yes. Hurry."

Jayden repositioned herself and unbuttoned her slacks and tugged them off her. Then she tossed them aside and crawled up between her legs, inching her way closer by wrapping her arms around her thighs and pulling on her. She snuck her tongue out and traced around the lacy rim of her panties, causing her to squirm and sigh in pleasure.

"Jayden," she said. "Put your mouth on me. Please. Agh. Yes. Put your mouth on me."

Jayden flattened her tongue and licked her hard from her moist hole beneath the fabric up to her hardened clit, struggling for freedom.

Kassandra lifted her head and shoulders. "Oh, God. Oh, God!"

Jayden reached up and played with her nipples. Kassandra took her hand, kissed it wildly, sucked on her fingers. The sensation sent Jayden into overdrive, and she licked her hard, flat clit again and again. Kassandra tensed each time there was contact, shuddering more and more. She clenched Jayden's hair and tried to force her to stay at her hungry flesh so she could explode and spill over. But Jayden fought her, milking her desire as best she could. Stopping to rim the lace of her panties once again, sneaking her tongue under every once in a while, to hear her cry out.

"I love you, Kassandra," Jayden said, turning her head to rub her cheekbone against her hot flesh, heating right through the moist fabric.

"Wha?" Kassandra sounded breathless. She opened her eyes and stared.

"I love you." Jayden bit her protruding clit, just enough to make her buck. "I love every last inch of you. I need you to know."

Kassandra tugged on her hair. "I love you, too, Jayden Beaumont." She laughed, her voice nearly hoarse. "I think I fell for you the moment you came on to me."

Jayden grinned. "I felt you," she said. "I felt you react to me."

"You did?"

"Yes. And I meant every word I said. Now more than ever. No one has ever moved me like you, Kassandra. No one. It's like you walked in from heaven. Just breezed right into my life, white light shining behind you."

Kassandra tugged on her again. "Come here." Jayden crawled to her and they kissed, hot and languid, deep and searching. Kassandra clung to her, nails digging in. Then she lowered her hand and slipped it beneath Jayden's shorts. Jayden closed her eyes, unable to move to stop her. Memories of Kassandra's delicate fingers playing her, swam through her, warming her. Her clit was already full when Kassandra found her.

"Oh fuck," Jayden groaned.

"Touch me," Kassandra said. "And kiss me while we touch each other. Slide your tongue in my mouth like how your fingers are sliding along my clit. I want to come while we are kissing."

Jayden hurriedly lowered her hand and slid it under Kassandra's panties. She found her incredibly slick and ready for her. Kassandra called her name when she ran her fingertips around and over her clit, once, twice, three times. When her chest and face bloomed in red splotches, Jayden slowed, kissed her, and framed her clit to stroke up and down. Their tongues met and danced, twirled, and stroked. They moved their fingers slow at first, teasing, sliding, gliding. And then when Jayden felt so full of desire she'd burst, she kissed her harder, delved deeper with her tongue, and slid her fingertips around and over her clit again.

Kassandra matched her, groaning into her. Jayden pumped her hips into her hand, clenched her eyes, so overcome with the reality that she was about to come with Kassandra, that she was feeling her beneath her fingers, that she nearly cried, she was so happy. She made a small noise, one that made Kassandra move faster, harder, and when she finally stiffened, shuddered, and cried out in Jayden's mouth, Jayden did the same, calling out into her mouth, hungry tongues still at it, slipping and sliding, starving. They moaned, pulsed, and stroked together, coming into the universe, soul to soul.

Jayden played her clit until she could take no more of Kassandra doing the same to her. She collapsed next to her and their hands stilled, chests heaving. Jayden laughed, incredulous, moved beyond words. She couldn't stop smiling. Next to her, Kassandra wiped tears. Jayden rolled toward her.

"Hey, you okay?" She stroked her soft cheek. Her eyes were crystal green as if just having purged all that was painful and wrong.

"God, yes. I'm really fucking great."

Jayden smiled softly. "You're beautiful," she said. "Like this. Right at this moment. Perfect. I wish I could capture it."

"Lucky for you you'll get to see a lot more of it."

Jayden warmed. "Yes, that is lucky for me. I'm the luckiest woman in the world."

Kassandra touched her face in return. "You're everything I didn't know I wanted."

"Here's to just being friends," Jayden said.

Kassandra punched her. "Smart-ass." Then she kissed her softly, and then deeper. "Here's to just being friends."

They kissed again and Jayden scooted lower, a hunger still eating at her insides. Quickly, she crawled over Kassandra's leg and settled between them. Kassandra laughed, already playing with Jayden's hair.

"What are you doing?"

"Giving you the full treatment, so to speak." Jayden lowered and breathed up her sensitive skin, causing her to jerk and shake.

"Jay-den," she breathed. "Don't tease me anymore. I can't take it."

"You want me to lick you now?"

"Ye-es. God, yes. Please."

Jayden kissed her lightly and then eased down her panties. She inhaled her deeply and snuck out her tongue. She licked her outer lips and then swirled, circling closer and closer to her clit. Kassandra's eyes fell closed and she tangled her fingers in Jayden's hair.

"Yes," she said again and again. "Oh, God, yes. Please, Jayden."

Jayden took her cue and flicked her clit, sending Kassandra into a wild spasm. She tugged and tore at Jayden, thrusting her hips upward.

"Please, Jayden, please. Make me come. I want to come in your mouth."

Jayden smothered her clit then, pressing and licking and slightly sucking. Kassandra nearly screamed as she held fast to her, bucking like a mad woman.

"Feels so good, feels so good. Jayden!" And she came, bolting up off the bed to a sitting position where she clung to Jayden and rubbed herself into her again and again. "Don't stop, don't stop—oh God, Jayden!" And she came again, this time long and deep, and she collapsed back and pulsed into Jayden, eyes trained on her ceiling, mouth open, neck strained.

"I love you," she said. "I love you."

Jayden gave until she stilled completely and yanked her head away. Jayden covered her pulsing flesh with her palm and rose to rest on her heaving breast. She kissed her lightly, all the way up to her ear where she whispered, "I love you, too."

Kassandra wiped tears and turned to snuggle into her. "Oh, God, Beaumont. If I had known you could do that, I would've given you the green light a long time ago."

Jayden laughed and held her tighter. "There's so much more than that to come," she said, not quite sure she could wait to show her.

"Jesus, will we ever leave the bedroom?"

"Not if you don't want to."

Kassandra kissed her neck. Licked her skin. "I don't want to."

Jayden rolled into her and pinned her down. "Good."

CHAPTER TWENTY-NINE

December brought temperatures in the sixties, and Angel's Wings was all abuzz with holiday business. Kassandra walked next to Jayden, holding her hand while some of the teens walked around them, holding long leashes led by numerous dogs. Dax and Lula were at the head of the pack, walking slowly, stopping here and there to sniff. With the cooler weather, the staff kept the dogs outdoors as much as possible, teaching them leash training and walking manners.

"Lula doesn't quite know what to do with all this land," Jayden said, squinting into the low sun.

"I don't either," Kassandra said. "It's so freeing. And I love the way the desert smells in the early morning."

Jayden pulled her close. "Well, you know, you can experience that any time you want. Every morning if you want."

They'd talked about moving in together before, but Jayden didn't push, and Kassandra appreciated that. She had just put in her notice with her job, and big changes were starting soon. She wasn't sure if she could handle another just yet. But the thought of living with Jayden, of waking up next to her every morning…she loved that thought. She loved how it made her heat from the inside out.

"Maybe soon," she said, causing Jayden to smile. "After all, I need a big wall to hang that painting Billy did for me."

"True."

They walked on, hiking through the back of the property. Every once in a while, Dax would trot back to make sure they were still there, then he'd return to the front. Jayden just laughed and shook her head. "Ever the protector," she said.

"He reminds me of you," Kassandra said. "He makes me feel loved, safe."

Jayden smiled. "I always want you to feel that way."

"I do. Every day now."

Jayden squeezed her and kissed her softly. The teens all groaned.

"Get a room!"

Kassandra laughed and her cheeks burned with embarrassment. Next to her, Tony ran up and grabbed her hand. He was beaming and he'd apparently just run full-sprint from the office.

"Guess what?" he said. "Guess freaking what?"

Kassandra had no idea, but by the look on his face, she knew it was good.

"What?"

"I got into that school. The special one. The trade school."

Kassandra and Jayden stopped. "Really?" He'd been wanting this for weeks now. "Tony, that's great!"

"I know, I know. I can learn engines, Ms. H. Be a real mechanic. Actually do something instead of sit in the learning center. I'm gonna be somebody."

Kassandra hugged him and held him tight. "You already are, Tony. You already are." She pulled away and wiped a tear from his cheek. "Are you still going to work here?"

"I can on weekends. My fosters don't want the long drive from the school to here during the week."

Kassandra looked to Jayden, who shrugged. "Fine by me. Go for it, kid."

Tony hopped up and down. "I gotta go tell Gus and Billy." He took off toward the head of the group.

"He sure is happy," Jayden said.

"Yes, he is."

"And that makes you happy," Jayden said.

"Yes, it does."

"Does he know you called in a reference?"

"No. And he doesn't know you did either."

Jayden smiled. "He'll thrive there."

"I think so, too."

Jayden kissed her neck. "Know what makes me happy?"

Kassandra blushed again as they walked pressed to one another. "I have some idea."

"Yeah?"

"Uh-huh. It involves sneaking off to the house."

"Mmm, yes. What do you say?"

Kassandra stared off into the setting sun and the plumes of bursting pink and purple. "Only if I get to do you."

Jayden laughed. "No way."

Kassandra shrugged. "Okay then, I'm happy walking." She was addicted to Jayden's taste, the feel of her flesh under her tongue, the hot slickness she loved to lap. And when she came beneath her, in her mouth, it was nothing short of earth-shattering. How had she lived so long without knowing, without loving?

Jayden groaned. "Fine. But it's my turn later."

Kassandra smiled, pleased with her short victory. "Okay then."

Jayden yanked on her hand and they hurried to the house. The teens laughed beyond them and some of them whistled.

"We're just checking on things," Kassandra called out.

But they knew better, and every single one of them seemed more than happy with the blooming relationship.

Jayden tugged on her again, and Kassandra ran after her up the steps to the door. She looked behind them at the setting sun and took a moment to thank her lucky stars. She had a wonderful, beautiful life. A life she could've never imagined.

And it had all started with a few life-altering words.

I want to read the book of your life. From page one until infinity.

About the Author

Ronica Black lives in the desert Southwest with her menagerie of animals and her menagerie of art. When she's not writing, she's still creating, whether that be drawing, painting, or woodworking. She loves long walks into the sunset, rescuing animals, anything pertaining to art, and spending time with those she loves. When she can, she enjoys returning to her roots in North Carolina, where she can sit on the front porch with her family, catch up on all the gossip, and enjoy a nice cold Cheerwine.

Ronica is a two- time Golden Literary Society winner and a three-time finalist for the Lambda Literary Awards.

Books Available From Bold Strokes Books

Change in Time by Robyn Nyx. Working in the past is hell on your future. The Extractor series: Book Two. (978-162639-880-1)

Love After Hours by Radclyffe. When Gina Antonelli agrees to renovate Carrie Longmire's new house, she doesn't welcome Carrie's overtures at friendship or her own unexpected attraction. A Rivers Community Novel. (978-163555-090-0)

Nantucket Rose by CF Frizzell. Maggie Jordan can't wait to convert a historic Nantucket home into a B&B, but doesn't expect to fall for mariner Ellis Chilton, who has more claim to the house than Maggie realizes. (978-163555-056-6)

Picture Perfect by Lisa Moreau. Falling in love wasn't supposed to be part of the stakes for Olive and Gabby, rival photographers in the competition of a lifetime. (978-162639-975-4)

Set the Stage by Karis Walsh. Actress Emilie Danvers takes the stage again in Ashland, Oregon, little realizing that landscaper Arden Philips is about to offer her a very personal romantic lead role. (978-163555-087-0)

Strike a Match by Fiona Riley. When their attempts at matchmaking fizzle out, firefighter Sasha and reluctant millionairess Abby find themselves turning to each other to strike a perfect match. (978-162639-999-0)

The Price of Cash by Ashley Bartlett. Cash Braddock is doing her best to keep her business afloat, stay out of jail, and avoid Detective Kallen. It's not working. (978-162639-708-8)

Under Her Wing by Ronica Black. At Angel's Wings Rescue, dogs are usually the ones saved, but when quiet Kassandra Haden meets outspoken owner Jayden Beaumont, the two stubborn women just might end up saving each other. (978-163555-077-1)

Underwater Vibes by Mickey Brent. When Hélène, a translator in Brussels, Belgium, meets Sylvie, a young Greek photographer and swim coach, unsettling feelings hijack Hélène's mind and body—even her poems. (978-163555-002-3)

A Date to Die by Anne Laughlin. Someone is killing people close to Detective Kay Adler, who must look to her own troubled past for a suspect. There she finds more than one person seeking revenge against her. (978-163555-023-8)

Captured Soul by Laydin Michaels. Can Kadence Munroe save the woman she loves from a twisted killer, or will she lose her to a collector of souls? (978-162639-915-0)

Dawn's New Day by TJ Thomas. Can Dawn Oliver and Cam Cooper, two women who have loved and lost, open their hearts to love again? (978-163555-072-6)

Definite Possibility by Maggie Cummings. Sam Miller is just out for good times, but Lucy Weston makes her realize happily ever after is a definite possibility. (978-162639-909-9)

Eyes Like Those by Melissa Brayden. Isabel Chase and Taylor Andrews struggle between love and ambition from the writers' room on one of Hollywood's hottest TV shows. (978-163555-012-2)

Heart's Orders by Jaycie Morrison. Helen Tucker and Tee Owens escape hardscrabble lives to careers in the Women's Army Corps, but more than their hearts are at risk as friendship blossoms into love. (978-163555-073-3)

Hiding Out by Kay Bigelow. Treat Dandridge is unaware that her life is in danger from the murderer who is hunting the woman she's falling in love with, Mickey Heiden. (978-162639-983-9)

Omnipotence Enough by Sophia Kell Hagin. Can the tiny tool that abducted war veteran Jamie Gwynmorgan accidentally acquires help her escape an unknown enemy to reclaim her stolen life and the woman she deeply loves? (978-163555-037-5)

Lessons in Desire by MJ Williamz. Can a summer love stand a four-month hiatus and still burn hot? (978-163555-019-1)